A Treasury
of Wise Action

A Treasury of Wise Action

Jataka Tales
of Compassion and Wisdom

Dharma Publishing

TALES OF COMPASSION AND WISDOM SERIES

A Treasury of Wise Action

LIBRARY OF CONGRESS CATALOGING IN PUBLICATION DATA

A treasury of wise action : Jataka tales of compassion
and wisdom.
     p.   cm. – (Tales of compassion and wisdom series)
     ISBN 0-89800-224-9 (pbk. : acid-free paper)
     1. Jataka stories, English. 2. Buddhist stories.
I. Dharma Publishing. II. Series
BQ1032.T74   1993
294.3'823–dc20
93-883 AC

Illustrations by Rosalyn White

Editing and design by Dharma Publishing
Typeset in ITC Bookman Light with
New Aster Outline initials
Printed and bound in the USA by Dharma Press

07 05 03 01 99 97 95 93   9 8 7 6 5 4 3 2 1

CONTENTS

v

Contents

PUBLISHER'S INTRODUCTION

The folktales in this collection have been beloved by millions of people, young and old, in India and Asia for more than 2,500 years. Through the actions of heroic animals and human beings, these stories celebrate the power of compassion, love, wisdom, and kindness. They teach that everything we do profoundly affects the quality of our lives. Selfish words and deeds bring unhappiness to us and to those around us while virtuous actions untainted by personal concerns give rise to goodness of such power that it uplifts all forms of life.

First told by the Buddha to clarify which attitudes and actions develop compassion and wisdom, these treasured accounts became known as Jatakas, or 'birth stories'. Carried down through the centuries, they have retained their popularity as vehicles for demonstrating the boundless benefit of positive thought and action.

Stories of saintly animals, high-minded kings, and wise merchants may at first seem to belong only to the realm of fables. We are not accustomed to believe in heroes so wise and noble that their actions have only positive effects. Is it possible that the compassionate actions of these ancient heroes could inspire us in our daily lives?

By their actions, the great-spirited heroes of these stories transform difficult situations and create new dimensions of harmony in the world. In the story of King Banyan Deer, the Deer King offers his own life to save the life of a pregnant doe. Overcome with admiration for this selfless action, the king not only saves the lives of both deer but also grants the Deer King's request that he give up hunting altogether.

Yet the story does not end here. When farmers seek to protect their crops from the freely roaming deer, the Deer King, motivated by compassion for all, effortlessly finds a way to bring the situation into harmony and balance.

Story after story encourages us to listen to our hearts, to deeply admire acts of wisdom, and to act, like the heroes of these stories, with love, compassion, and joy. These are stories to read with an open heart, attuned to the knowledge they awaken within us.

Introduction

All of us face difficult times, particularly now when the need for both individual and global transformation is so urgent. When we are worried, uneasy, and beset by problems, the teaching that these tales have to offer may bring us great benefit. Knowing that openhearted action for the benefit of others will bring positive results, we can choose to move toward what we hold most dear and discover for ourselves the positive consequences of our actions.

The Jataka emblem which appears on the cover of this book and as the logo for this series can help to remind us of the value of the ancient wisdom which calls us to develop a deeper and wiser perspective. The attitudes and views that grow from this deeper perspective can guide us to discover our own fulfillment today. In the story represented by this emblem, four good friends choose wisdom as their guide to a harmonious life. Like many of the stories in this collection, the tale is disarmingly simple, but upon reflection its deeper meaning shines through to inform our lives. Since this story is not included elsewhere in this collection, it is narrated briefly here:

Once, under a great banyan tree on the slopes of the Himalayas, there lived four good friends—a partridge, a rabbit, a monkey, and an elephant. But as time went on, they began to treat each other without kindness or respect. They quarrelled and complained, and their daily lives grew very dissatisfying.

One day they decided that they needed a wise elder to advise and guide them. They agreed to find out who among them was the oldest and to honor that one as their counselor.

"Friends," said the elephant, "when I was a baby, I could walk over to this banyan tree and tickle my belly with its topmost branches. I've known this tree since it was a sapling."

"My friends," the monkey said, "when I was small, I could sit on the ground and eat the topmost leaves of this banyan tree. I've known this tree since it was a bush."

"Friends," the rabbit said, "when I was a youngster, I could nibble the topmost leaves of this banyan tree. I've known this tree since it was just a small sprig!"

"My friends," said the partridge, "long ago there grew another great banyan tree far from here. I ate its fruits and carried seeds to this very spot. From one of those seeds, this great tree grew."

The elephant, the monkey, and the rabbit agreed. "Friend, you are the oldest among us.

From this time on, you will instruct us wisely, and we will honor and respect you."

In this way, the lives of the partridge, the rabbit, the monkey, and the elephant were soon restored to harmony and joy.

While based on traditional accounts, the stories in this collection have been adapted for the children of today. Since 1971, Dharma Publishing has published twenty Jataka Tales for young children in The Jataka Tales Series. Many of our readers have requested an anthology of Jataka tales suitable for older children, and this book, part of a new series entitled Tales of Compassion and Wisdom, is offered particularly to children between the ages of 9 and 12.

We wish to offer special thanks to Karabi Sen, who as a child in her native Bengal heard many Jataka tales passed down through the accomplished Bengali storytelling tradition. She has shared these tales with American children, and we are grateful to her for her versions of eight of the stories included here: How the Poor Traveler Became Rich, The Crocodile and the Gorilla, The Kingshuk Tree and the Four Princes, The Monster of the Lotus Lake, The Lion's Skin, The Turtle and the Swans, The Woodcutter King, and The Serpent and His Jewel.

We hope that young readers of these stories will hear them in their hearts and express their inspiration in action. The book is dedicated to every child who aspires to positive action informed by compassion and wisdom.

A Treasury
of Wise Action

KING BANYAN DEER

Once upon a time in a deep forest near the ancient city of Benares there lived a deer named Banyan. His rich coat was golden like the sun, his antlers shone like polished silver, and his eyes were like round jewels, alight with love toward all creatures. His body was as large as a colt's and on his four powerful legs he could run like the wind. Banyan was a King of Deer—indeed he watched over a herd of five hundred deer. His subjects loved and respected him because he was a kind leader and wise teacher.

In the nearby forest another herd of five hundred deer was led by another golden deer named Branch. Branch often visited King Banyan Deer to ask his advice and counsel.

Reigning over the animals of the forest and every person in the land was the powerful King of Benares. He commanded an army of thousands and was a fierce warrior himself. But he was also a fair and just leader who upheld the laws of the land. His subjects obeyed him out of both fear and respect.

The king had one demand which was met without question: Every day of the year fresh meat, roasted to perfection, was to be served to him for dinner. The king was especially fond of venison or deer meat.

Each morning after he had finished meeting with his ministers of state, the king would mount his horse and go out into the forest to hunt. Since it was difficult to find a deer in the large forest, the king commanded the people from the towns and villages to go into the forest ahead of him to drive the deer out of their lairs. Every morning farmers would drop their plows, craftsmen would lay down their tools, and bakers would leave their cooking fires unattended to accompany the king into the forest.

Although the people disliked having to stop their work to help the king hunt, they were afraid to complain.

One morning as a young girl watched her father and twenty other men go off into the forest, she said to her mother, "Why do the people drive the deer to the king each day? Why not drive the deer into the king's pleasure garden? Then the king could easily shoot a deer whenever he pleased without bothering anyone else."

"Yes!" her mother responded excitedly. "We can plant fine grass for the deer to eat and there is already a stream of fresh water flowing through the park. Although we cannot save the deer from being hunted, at least we can save ourselves from having to hunt every day."

By the end of the day all the villagers and townspeople knew of the young girl's plan. Early the next morning, every man, woman, boy, and girl old enough to walk went into the forest to find the deer, armed with sticks and many kinds of weapons. They formed a circle three miles wide in order to catch the deer within the perimeter. In so doing, they encircled the area where the Banyan and Branch deer lived with their herds.

As soon as the king's subjects saw the deer, they beat the trees, bushes, and ground with their sticks until they drove the herds out into the open. Then they rattled their swords and spears and bows, waving their arms and making such a great noise that they were able to drive the deer into the pleasure garden. Then they closed the garden gates.

Just as the high gates were closing, the king arrived at the pleasure garden. "Sire," said the young girl, making a deep curtsy, "no longer will you need to roam the forest in search of deer for your table. We have driven a great herd of deer into your pleasure garden where you can easily hunt them whenever you wish."

The king looked in astonishment at the young girl, then slowly smiled. "You have done well," he said. Then without a moment's hesitation the king entered the pleasure garden with his followers, an arrow notched in his bow.

There among the deer he saw what looked at first like patches of sunlight. Looking closer, he made out two large golden deer, King Banyan Deer and Branch Deer, moving among the herd. Never before had he seen creatures of such majestic beauty. "From this day forth," he commanded, "on pain of death, no one shall harm these two magnificent golden deer!"

With that, he aimed at a doe who was standing timidly nearby. Before the doe could flee the king's arrow struck her in the side, lodging deep between two ribs. Stunned but not killed, the doe stumbled into the bushes and collapsed in great pain. The king's second arrow felled a buck which was dragged away to the king's kitchen.

Sometimes the king would go to the pleasure garden and shoot the deer; sometimes his cook would go in his place. As the weeks passed, many deer were wounded and died in great pain. Finally King Banyan Deer called the herds together, saying, "Friends, we know that we cannot escape death, but let us not continue to suffer wounds needlessly. Let the deer take turns going to the block, one day one from my herd and the next day one from the herd of Branch Deer. This way we will not have to bear the pain of being injured or crippled."

The deer willingly agreed to this plan. Each day the deer whose turn it was would walk to the gate of the pleasure garden, lay its head down on a chopping block, and wait for the blow to fall.

One day the lot fell on a pregnant doe from Branch Deer's herd. Afraid for her unborn child, the doe went to Branch Deer and begged that she be passed over until after her fawn was born.

Although Branch Deer felt pity for the doe, he said, "Your lot was chosen and you must go. If I passed you over all the other deer would find some reason to be passed over as well."

Despairing, the doe went to King Banyan Deer. "Your majesty, " she said, "the lot has fallen on me today. I would willingly take my turn just as the other deer have, but I am pregnant. Please let me take my turn later, after my fawn is born."

"Do not fear, little mother, your young one will be spared," King Banyan Deer answered gently. "Go rest in the gardens now. I will see that the turn passes over you today."

No sooner had the doe left him than King Banyan Deer went quietly to the place of execution and laid his head on the block. Minutes later, the king's cook appeared, knife in hand. Seeing the splendid golden deer ready for sacrifice, he cried out in alarm. "I dare not kill this golden deer whom the king ordered not to be harmed! The king must be told of this at once!"

Not knowing what to make of the cook's report, the King of Benares mounted his chariot and rode to the pleasure garden with a large following.

The king's heart skipped a beat when he saw the huge golden deer offering himself at the block. "My friend, King of the Deer, I granted you a life free from harm. How is it that you now lie on the block, ready to give your life?"

"Sire, a doe large with young begged that her life be spared until her fawn was born. Although I can not pass her fate on to another, I can take her fate upon myself."

"Golden creature," said the king, "never before have I seen one so full of compassion as you—not among men or beasts. I am pleased with you beyond measure. Arise! I will spare both your life and hers!"

King Banyan Deer stood up slowly, and the warmth from his compassionate heart radiated in all directions. "Though two are spared, what shall the rest do, O king of men?" he asked sweetly and humbly.

"I will spare their lives also, Great One!" said the king.

"Sire, only the deer in your pleasure garden will thus be safe. What shall all the rest do?"

"Their lives too I will spare," answered the king.

"Sire, deer will thus be free from harm, but what will the rest of the four-footed creatures do?"

"Their lives I shall also spare," replied the king.

"Sire, four-footed creatures will thus be safe, but what will flocks of birds do?"

"I will spare all their lives," the king said quietly, feeling compassion stir within his heart.

"Sire, birds will thus be safe, but what will the fish in the great waters do?"

"Great teacher, the fish shall also be spared— all creatures of the land, sea, and sky will I spare from this day forth."

After helping the King of Benares to understand compassion, King Banyan Deer said, "Rule virtuously and wisely, great leader. Instill harmony and peace in all your subjects—men, women, children, and beasts of the land, sea, and sky. Thus when your own life passes on you will enter the bliss of heaven."

With the grace and charm that marks an enlightened being, the Banyan Deer thus taught the king the ways of compassion. For a few more days he remained in the pleasure garden teaching the king, and then he and his herd passed freely into the forest once again.

In a few weeks the doe brought forth a fawn as fair as the opening lotus bud. Seeing that her young one chose to play with the Branch deer, his mother said, "My child, make friends among the Banyan deer as well, for their company can bring you only good fortune." And to inspire him she sang this song:

"Honor the Banyan deer;
make them the friends of your heart.
Their king was willing to die for us.
From that love we are never apart."

King Banyan's work was far from done, however. Having been granted immunity from harm, the deer grew accustomed to eating the farmers' crops. The farmers dared not hit them or drive them away because they remembered the decree that no creature was to be harmed. So they assembled in the King of Benares' courtyard and laid the matter before him.

"When the Banyan Deer offered himself as sacrifice, he taught me a great lesson," said the King of Benares. "In return I made promises which I will keep at all cost. Not a single person in my kingdom may harm the deer. Now go!"

When King Banyan Deer heard this news he called his herd together and said, "You must not eat the farmers' crops. We have plenty of food in the forest and wild fields." The herd agreed to leave the farmers' fields alone from that time forward.

Having thus spoken to his followers, King Banyan Deer sent a message to the farmers, saying, "From now on let no farmer fence his field, but merely mark its boundaries with leaves tied up round it."

And so, we are told, began a custom of tying up leaves to indicate a field's boundaries, and never was a deer known to trespass on a field marked in this way. For thus had they been instructed in ages past by the great teacher, King Banyan Deer.

11

THE ELEPHANT
AND THE KING

L ong ago, high on the slopes of the Himalayas in Northern India was a hill called Chandagiri. On the side of the hill were woods filled with thousands of flowering and fruitbearing trees. Among the trees were secluded lotus pools and retreats far from the places where humans dwelt.

A large herd of elephants lived on the hill. Among them was born a fine young elephant, his head the color of seashells, his body as strong and white as the lotus. When he grew up, he looked after his blind, aged mother with love and respect. He gave her food and drink before he himself ate and drank. He groomed and cleaned his mother's tall body with the ivy that grew in the forest. And so this young elephant looked after his mother with kindness and great affection.

After he had groomed his mother and served her food, and had guided her into the shade to lie down, he would often go off to roam with the other elephants. One day some hunters who were following the chase saw him and told the king of Kashi about him.

"Your majesty," they said, "there is a young elephant living in the forest who is so handsome that he is a fitting mount for your majesty."

The king decided that he wanted this elephant for himself. So he went to the forest with one hundred strong soldiers and caught the young elephant. "This will be a splendid riding animal for me," thought the king.

The king brought the elephant to Benares and put him in the royal stables. There he gave him sweet grass and hay and offered him food and water from his own hand. But the elephant would not eat or drink, refusing even the finest foods. He could think only of his blind old mother, alone now in the forest. He sighed deeply, wept, and grew thinner each day.

"Noble elephant," the king said, "I offer you the best food and the purest water, yet you do not eat or drink. I surround you with other fine elephants, yet you are not happy. How can I satisfy you? I have jewels and gold and fine silks to adorn you. What is it you want?"

The young elephant replied in human speech, "Your majesty, food and drink cannot please me, nor can jewels or riches bring me joy. My mother lives in the forest, and she is old and blind. Ever since I can remember I have given food and drink to my mother before eating myself. Though I die here, I resolve not to take food or drink again without giving some to my mother."

The king of Kashi was a kind man, and the elephant's words touched him deeply. He thought, "It is wonderful that this young elephant is so devoted to his mother, so just and noble that during all these many days he has not touched either food or drink because of his grief for her. There are not many humans with such compassion and concern for others. We should not bring this noble elephant to any harm."

Then he said to his chief ministers, "Let this young elephant go free. Let him return to the woods from which we took him. It would be wrong for us to keep him apart from his old mother and let him die here." And so at the king's command the elephant was led to the borders of the forest and set free.

Immediately the young elephant began to search for his mother. Although food and water were plentiful in the forest, he did not stop to eat or drink. His only thought was to find his mother.

15

He searched high and low, but he could not find her in any of her favorite places. Determined not to rest until he found her, he climbed to the top of a hill and uttered a loud roar. He listened intently but heard no response. He roared again, this time more loudly than before. A faint cry rose up from the foot of the hill. His mother had heard her son's roar and cried out in reply.

The young elephant followed his mother's voice to a pool of water. There she lay, too weak to move, covered with mud and mire. Tenderly, her son broke off some nearby vines and used them to wipe the mire from her body. Then he filled his trunk with water from the pool and joyfully washed her. His joy in caring for her was so great that his heart glowed like a radiant sun. Waves of love and happiness spread out in all directions.

As she became spotless and clean, his joy grew so great he thought his heart would burst. Miraculously, as he bathed her eyes, her sight returned. "My son," she cried out in amazement, "what joy to see you again!"

Bathed in wonder like a sweet nectar, they could not decide whether to laugh or cry. Gently the young elephant told his mother everything that had happened—how he had been captured and taken to Benares, and how he had been offered royal wealth and splendor. He told her of the king's kindness in letting him return to the forest.

"My son," his mother said, "I wish that all who are needy may have loyal protectors like you! The world delights in the greatness of your virtue. May the compassionate King of Kashi and his people rejoice just as I rejoice today at the sight of my noble son."

THE KING'S CHARGER

Once upon a time in Benares a thoroughbred horse of splendid qualities was chosen to be the king's special charger. Surrounded by luxury, he was fed on the finest rice, which was always served to him in a golden dish worth a hundred thousand coins. The ground of his stall was perfumed with exquisite scents, and crimson curtains were hung from its walls. Overhead hung a canopy studded with stars of gold. The stall was decorated with wreaths and garlands of fragrant flowers, and a lamp fed with scented oil was always burning.

The king of Benares was renowned for his kindness and wisdom and his people enjoyed great wealth and prosperity. Seven neighboring kingdoms were also thriving and prosperous, but their kings envied the great wealth of Benares and plotted to take its riches for their own. One day the kings of these seven kingdoms surrounded

19

Benares and sent this message to the king: "Either surrender your kingdom or fight." After assembling his ministers, the king of Benares presented the matter to them and asked for their advice.

The king's ministers said, "You should not go out to do battle in person, sire. Dispatch your most valiant knight to fight them first; later on, if he fails, we will decide what to do."

Then the king sent for that knight and said to him, "Can you fight the seven kings, my brave knight?"

"Give me your noble charger, sire, and then I can fight not only seven kings but all the kings in India," said the knight.

"My noble knight, take my charger or any other horse you please, and do battle for the kingdom of Benares."

"Very good, my sovereign lord," said the knight, and with a bow he left the upper chambers of the palace.

The knight had the noble charger led out and sheathed in mail, armed himself as well from head to toe, and fastened on his sword. Then, mounting the noble steed, he rode out of the city gate.

With a lightning charge he entered the first camp, throwing it into confusion. The frightened armies tried to press forward here and retreat there, but they were no match for the peerless knight and his great-hearted charger. Taking the first king alive, the knight brought him back to Benares a prisoner to be placed in the soldiers' custody.

Returning to the field, he lifted his shining sword overhead and charged the second camp. Overtaking all who challenged him, he took the second camp and then the third. Without pausing to rest, he pierced the ranks of the fourth and fifth camps and did not stop until he had captured five kings alive. He had just overtaken the sixth camp and had captured the sixth king when the charger was wounded by an arrow. Blood streamed from the wound, and the noble animal cried out in pain.

Seeing that the charger was wounded, the knight rode back to the gates of Benares and dismounted, then commanded the horse to lie down. As he loosened the charger's mail he thought, "No other mount can match the courage and endurance of this noble steed. But against all odds I will do battle for my king." He called for another horse and set about arming it.

As the noble charger lay at full length on his side, he opened his eyes and watched what the knight was doing. "The horse that my rider is arming will not be able to break down the seventh camp and capture the seventh king," he thought. "All that we have gained will be lost. This valiant knight will be slain, and the king, too, will fall into the hands of the enemy. Although weakened by loss of blood, I will use my last strength to protect the welfare of Benares and my virtuous king."

The wounded charger called out to the knight, "Valiant knight, we both know that even though I am injured, I am the only horse able to penetrate the seventh camp and capture the seventh king. We cannot lose what we have gained; have me set upon my feet and clad again in armor. I have the strength to bear you once more into battle. Together we will be victorious."

So the knight had the charger set upon his feet, bound up his wound, and strapped his armor upon him. Without hesitation the charger carried the knight straight into the midst of the seventh camp where the few who dared to challenge them were quickly defeated. The knight brought back the seventh king alive and placed him in the custody of the king's soldiers.

Then the soldiers led the noble horse up to the king's gate, where the seven captured kings stood awaiting their fate. The king came out to look upon the charger and the captive kings. Clad in shining armor, the great-hearted charger spoke to his sovereign:

"O magnanimous king, today you shine with illustrious glory and the lives of your rival kings rest in your hands. Grant me these requests so that I may rest in peace: Do not kill these seven kings or enslave their people. Bind them by an oath, and let them go back to their kingdoms. Let this valiant knight enjoy all the honor due to us both. As for yourself, may you always rule in charity and generosity, and justly protect the welfare of your people."

The king of Benares listened carefully to these words and promised to abide by them for the rest of his days. Then the soldiers began to take off the charger's mail. While they were removing it piece by piece, the noble steed died peacefully.

Having witnessed the great charger's sacrifice and struck with wonder at his compassion and wisdom, the seven captured kings sank to their knees and vowed never again to allow greed and envy to lead them to war. They promised to live in peace with the kingdom of Benares and to teach the way of peace to all their subjects.

The king had the charger's body cremated with great respect, bestowed honor on the knight, and sent the seven kings back to their homes. Thus the king honored the charger's selfless action, in which he offered his life so that all the rulers and their subjects would learn to live together in harmony.

THE MERCHANT
WHO PERSEVERED

L ong ago a wise and compassionate child was born into the family of a merchant. When he grew up, he became a merchant himself and traveled all around India with five hundred carts of goods. He took with him one thousand men and women to handle the goods and tend the oxen who pulled the carts. His caravan carried exotic spices, pickled herbs, handsome wool rugs, embroidered silks, copper pots, and other goods.

One day the caravan came to a large desert two hundred miles wide, with sand so fine that it slipped through the fingers of a closed fist. As soon as the sun came up the sand grew as hot as a bed of charcoal embers, and no one could walk on it. The heat of this desert was so intense no one could survive it for even a day without water.

People who wanted to cross the desert traveled at night and made sure to take water, firewood, oil, rice, and anything else they might need along the way. At dawn they would stop and make camp, arranging their carts in a circle and spreading an awning overhead to shield them from the sun. Then they would eat an early meal and rest in the shade all day long.

When the sun set, they had their evening meal. As soon as the sand became cool, they would yoke the oxen to their carts and move forward. Although the desert was as trackless as an ocean, they found their way with the help of a skilled desert pilot who used his knowledge of the stars to navigate the long stretches of sand.

In this way the merchant and his caravan crossed the desert. When there were only seven miles left to go, the merchant thought, "By dawn we'll be out of this desert and won't need the wood and water we are carrying."

After they had eaten their supper, he ordered the wood and water to be thrown away so the carts would be lighter. Yoking the carts, they set out across the desert once more. The pilot sat in the front cart, looking up at the sky and directing their course through the position of the stars.

The pilot had gone so long without sleep that he could barely keep his eyes open. He nodded off, then woke up again with a start. But try as he may, he could not keep his eyes from closing.

Soon he fell fast asleep and did not even notice when the oxen swung around and began retracing their steps into the desert.

All night long the oxen plodded steadily, moving further back into the desert. At dawn the pilot woke up, saw with alarm the position of the stars overhead, and shouted out, "Quickly! Turn the carts around! We're going in the wrong direction!"

As the carts were turning around and forming into line, the sun came up over the horizon. The people of the caravan looked around the desert. "This is where we camped yesterday," they cried. "All our wood and water are gone! Surely we will die! All is lost now!"

They arranged their carts in a circle, unyoked the oxen, and spread the awning overhead. Then everyone in the caravan, wailing in despair, flung themselves down in the shade of their carts.

The merchant thought, "It was a mistake to throw away our supplies, but if I give up, every single one of us will die." While it was still early and cool he walked out from the camp and looked around until he came upon a clump of kusha grass.

"This grass," he thought, "could only have grown here if there were water underneath it." So he ordered that ten men bring shovels and dig a hole at that spot. As the sun rose in the sky, the men dug and dug. They took turns digging until they had made a hole ten feet deep, but they did not find water. Several men collapsed in despair.

"You must not give up," said the merchant. "There is surely water at this spot—we have only to keep going and we will find it."

The men dug to twenty feet and then with a great effort, to thirty feet. The sun grew hotter and hotter. Without water to drink or cool their bodies, all of the men became exhausted and parched with thirst. At forty feet down the shovels struck a rock, and everyone lost heart.

The merchant, feeling sure there must be water under the rock, lowered himself down into the hole on a rope and stood on the rock. Stooping down, he put his ear on it and listened. Hearing the sound of water flowing underneath the rock, he climbed out of the hole and said to a young serving boy, the only digger remaining who had not given up in despair: "My boy, if you give up, we will all die. So take heart! I am too old to wield the sledge hammer—you must take it and strike the rock with all your might."

Knowing that there was no other hope, the boy went down into the hole and struck the rock with the heavy hammer. With his first stroke, the rock split in half and fell into the water below. As the boy scrambled up the rope the water lapped at his feet. It rose higher and higher until it reached the top of the hole.

All the people of the caravan drank the water and poured it over their bodies. Then they chopped up their spare axles and yokes and other surplus gear for firewood, cooked their rice and ate it, and fed their oxen. As soon as the sun set, they hoisted a flag next to the well and traveled on to the city that lay beyond the edge of the desert.

There they traded their goods for many times their value. "My friends," the merchant said, "you have shared the hardship of the desert with me, now share the bounty also! When we return to our homes, each of you will receive a share of this gold, for there is enough to make us all prosper!"

Then the servant boy quietly approached the merchant and said, "Good leader, your calmness and ingenuity saved all of our lives and now you have shared your gold with us as well. But beyond this you have taught me a lesson more valuable than gold. Following your example, I found the confidence to keep trying when everything appeared hopeless. Your perseverance has led us all to abundance and wisdom."

The merchant thanked the boy for his courage and understanding and they rode together as the caravan began its journey homeward.

HOW THE POOR TRAVELER BECAME RICH

Once upon a time there lived a successful merchant who knew how to take advantage of things that others might dismiss as completely useless. One morning when this merchant was walking down the street on his way to see the king, his eyes fell on a dead rat in a corner. He muttered to himself, "An honest, hardworking, clever person could make enough money even from a dead rat!"

Just at that moment, a young traveler who was poor but honest happened to be passing by. He overheard what the merchant said.

"Since I have nothing to lose, why don't I try my luck with the dead rat?" So the young man picked up the rat and went on his way.

Soon he came across a market where one of the merchants had a pet cat. The merchant was looking for some food for his cat, and seeing the rat, he bought it from the boy for a penny.

The young man now had a penny. With his penny he bought some brown sugar and an earthen pitcher. He filled the pitcher with water and sat by the path leading out of the forest, awaiting the return of the florists who made daily trips to the woods to gather flowers.

Every evening the flowersellers returned by the same path. As they emerged out of the forest, tired and thirsty, the young man gave each of them a glass of cool water sweetened with the brown sugar. In return, each of the florists offered him a bunch of flowers.

Later that evening the man went to the flower-market and sold the flowers. He now had enough money to buy food for himself and more brown sugar for the following day's business.

Late in the morning he went to the flowermarket with his pitcher of sugar water. It was almost noon, and the flowersellers were hot and thirsty. All the buying and selling and the dusty air had parched their throats, so they were glad to be able to pay for a drink with some leftover flowers and plants.

The young man covered these carefully with a damp cloth to keep them fresh. In the evening when the market opened again, he sold his flowers and plants for some more money. Within four or five days of business he was able to save eight silver coins.

A week later, a big storm hit the city, and a great number of broken branches, dry sticks, and twigs lay about in the king's garden. The gardener was trying to figure out how to clear this huge mess when the young man, who had observed his plight, came up to him. The young man offered to take care of the problem if the gardener would agree to give him all the wood. The gardener consented at once.

Then the clever young man took a bag of candy from his pocket and went to the street where some boys were playing. He gave some candy to the boys and, in turn, they gladly helped him clear the king's garden and gather all the wood into a big pile by the street.

The king's potter lived next to the royal garden. He needed to make a fire to bake clay but happened to be short of firewood. As soon as he stepped out on the road he saw the pile of wood and bought the entire lot. He was so glad to be saved the trip to the market that he gave the young man some of his big earthen pots in addition to sixteen silver coins for the wood.

The man now had twenty-four silver coins and began to think of some way to use this money to increase his wealth. He had been noticing for some time that every morning about five hundred grasscutters left the city to cut grass from neighboring fields. They tied the grass in neat bundles and brought them back to the city to sell at the royal stable.

A plan took form in the young man's mind. Just outside the city gates he dug some holes. In those holes he planted the huge pots that the potter had given him. He filled the pots with water and waited by the gate for the sun to set. At dusk the homebound grasscutters approached the gates and gladly accepted the cool water which the young man offered to them. He continued to serve water to the thirsty grasscutters evening after evening.

The grasscutters were so pleased with him that they wanted to give him something in return. The young man politely declined to take anything for offering plain water to thirsty people. However, he told the grasscutters that should the time come when he would need a favor from them, he would let them know. The grasscutters gladly agreed to this arrangement.

As the young man sat by the city gates he watched traders and merchants enter and leave the city. Soon he knew who everyone was and eventually made friends with them all. He became especially close to two merchants, one of whom traded by land, the other by sea.

One afternoon, the trader by land informed the young man that the following day a merchant would arrive in Benares with five hundred horses. Immediately the young man made plans.

When the grasscutters returned to the city that evening, he approached them with his request. He asked that each of the five hundred grasscutters spare him just one bundle of grass. He also asked that they not sell any grass at the city gates the following day until he had finished selling his. The grasscutters readily granted his request.

The following day, when the horse merchant arrived, he saw the young man sitting with five hundred neat bundles of freshly cut grass. Finding no one else willing to sell, the merchant bought all five hundred bundles for his five hundred horses. The merchant paid the young man two coins for each bundle of grass. The young man was overjoyed, for he now had one thousand coins!

A few months later, the merchant who traded by sea brought news that a large boat carrying all kinds of merchandise would arrive in Benares the next day. Again the young man lost no time in using this opportunity.

Early at dawn he rented a cart and left for the docks, where the boat had just anchored. He went inside the boat, bargained, and set a price for each of the commodities, putting down a deposit to show his good faith to buy. He made sure to mark each of the things with his seal, which was a ring with his name on it.

Then the young man came out of the boat and set up an attractive silk tent nearby on the bank of the Ganges. When passersby stopped to stare, he hired several of them to be his assistants. He rented fine uniforms for his assistants, and had them stand outside the tent where they made an impressive show. He left strict instructions that if merchants came to see him, they should be allowed inside the tent only one at a time.

As business hours drew near, the news spread about the arrival of a large merchant vessel. Soon nearly a hundred traders gathered at the docks to buy the goods.

But to their frustration they learned that a certain merchant had already purchased everything that the boat carried, all by himself! Hearing this, they began to look for this powerful merchant and soon came to the young man's tent. The stately tent and richly dressed servants greatly impressed them.

"He must be powerful indeed," they muttered to one another.

One at a time the traders met our young man and agreed to buy his merchandise. The price set for each article was, on average, one thousand coins more than what the young man had paid to the shipowner. At the end of the day he had sold the entire boatload of goods. After paying the shipowner what he owed him, for he had paid only a deposit before, the young man was two hundred thousand coins richer.

When he returned home that night he was so excited he could not sleep. As he lay awake, one by one he recalled the events that had led to his good fortune.

He thought of the days when he had no money. Then he remembered seeing the older merchant and overhearing his comments on the dead rat. He felt that he owed part of his success to this merchant's wise remark. Had it not been for those words of his about how an honest, hardworking person could make use of every opportunity, he would not have picked up the rodent. And that was how his good fortune began.

At daybreak, he took half of his profit and went to see the older merchant, for he wanted to share his fortune with him. The older trader received him graciously. When he had heard the entire story, he was amazed at the young man's enterprise and pleased with his honesty.

The merchant thought, "This young man is a jewel. No, he is more than that: He is a mine of virtue, wealth, and generosity. How could I let him go? I will offer to make him my business partner. I will even encourage my daughter to marry him so that she and all my family may benefit from his good qualities. As partners and members of the same family he and I can only increase our wealth and the extent of our good deeds; together we can bring great benefit to many people."

The merchant's daughter entered the room briefly with a tray of refreshments. The pomegranate color of her veil made her look very beautiful. One bashful look from her eyes, which were as dark as a pair of black bees, was enough to conquer the young man's heart. One glance from his eyes awakened her love and overcame her shyness.

As only fools put off auspicious moments and events, and as the merchant, his daughter, and the young merchant were all wise people, they immediately made plans for the young couple's marriage. The wedding took place soon after, and the young man and his bride lived happily together.

Since the older merchant had no sons, his daughter and his son-in-law inherited all his riches. They shared their wealth with the poor and needy, and inspired others by their example.

The power of the young man's resourceful and honest deeds brought him ever-increasing wealth and happiness which he and his wife shared with everyone they met. Their children and grandchildren did likewise, and their wealth continued to grow. In the same way the power of our good actions brings results which we can share with others. Like ripples spread outward from a stone dropped in water, the influence of good actions radiates far beyond us and touches the lives of future generations.

THE CROCODILE
AND THE GORILLA

Once upon a time, deep in the middle of a forest in the Himalayas, there lived a gorilla who was as strong as an elephant. His huge body was covered with soft, silky fur. All day long he romped about, swinging from tree to tree and eating ripe, juicy fruits.

Near this forest was a river where a crocodile lived with her mate. One fine day the crocodile was basking in the sun. As she lay on the warm sand, her eyes fell on the gorilla, who was sitting on the branch of a guava tree. He was nibbling on plump guavas and dangling his legs.

"What a handsome animal!" she thought. "I wish I could be strong like him!" Then she had an idea—"Well, perhaps I could be as strong as he is if I ate his heart!"

The crocodile told her mate about her wish. Day after day she talked to him about how much she wanted to be strong like the gorilla. Finally, one day he said: "It is not an easy task to get a gorilla's heart. He lives on land while you live in water. But if you must have his heart to eat you must find a way to get it!"

The crocodile made up her mind to get the gorilla's heart. She thought hard. At last she had a plan ready, and she set out to meet the gorilla. As she raised her head above the waters she saw the gorilla just a few feet across from her, drinking water from the river.

"Hello, Mr. Gorilla," she said, "how are you this morning?"

"Oh, just fine, I suppose," said the gorilla.

"Are you sure? You look pretty bored. Well, I can think of something fun for you to do."

"Really?" said the gorilla, suspiciously.

"Sure. Do you see the blue line on the other side of the river? That line is a forest of fruit trees. Mangoes and jackfruits, bananas and guavas grow there in abundance. The fruits are ripe and juicy, like the color of the sun. How happily the birds sing as they eat those fruits!"

"Is that so?" The gorilla was starting to dream.

"You know something?" said the crocodile. "I've never seen gorillas in that forest. I've seen little monkeys, but—gorillas? None at all. You will be the lord of that forest. You can eat the fruits and chase the birds and the monkeys as much as you like."

"But I don't swim. I can't cross the river to go to that lovely forest," sighed the gorilla.

"Well, if you climb on my back, I can carry you across the river. After all, what are friends for?" said the crocodile.

The gorilla agreed. Soon he was sailing across the river on the crocodile's back, heading towards the bank on the other side.

When they were halfway across the river, the crocodile suddenly dived under the water.

"Hey, what are you trying to do, drown me?" cried the gorilla.

At this, the crocodile burst out laughing. "Ha! Ha! My friend, did you really think that I cared for you so much that I would carry you on my back all the way across this enormous river, just so you can enjoy some fruits? I brought you here so that I can have your heart to eat," said the crocodile.

The gorilla saw that he had been tricked. Quickly he thought of a way to escape.

"Well, my friend, in that case you should have told me before about your plans. You will be very disappointed when you find there is no heart inside me. We gorillas do not carry our hearts around all the time. We jump around so much that we are afraid we will break our hearts, so we always hide our hearts in a safe place."

"Oh dear!" said the alarmed crocodile. "Now I'm in trouble." The crocodile thought for a while and then said to the gorilla, "Look, let's make a deal. If you give me your heart, I'll let you go. Now where is your heart?"

"That sounds like a fair deal to me," said the gorilla. "My heart is hidden in a yellow fruit. It hangs from the fig tree by the riverside. If you take me there I'll be glad to give you my heart."

The crocodile turned around and took the gorilla back to the riverbank. Quickly the gorilla climbed up the tree and looked down at the crocodile from between the clustering leaves of the fig tree. This time it was his turn to laugh.

"You stupid crocodile! You didn't really believe I would give you my heart, did you! Ha! Ha! If you are so greedy, eat your own heart out!"

Sadly, the crocodile lay down on the sand. Big tears trickled down from her eyes.

The gorilla felt sorry for the unhappy crocodile. "Why do you desire the heart of a gorilla?" he asked.

"Because I want to be strong like you, swinging from tree to tree, plucking fruit from the branches," she confessed.

"To be strong you need only feel content within your own heart. Wanting to be someone else will only bring you unhappiness. If you recognize the truth in what I am saying, you can go back home with confidence and learn to accept your own nature."

The crocodile recognized the truth in the gorilla's advice and went back home to put this advice to use. "From now on," she said to her mate, "I will find the strength I need within my own heart!"

THE FOOLISH MONKEYS

Once upon a time a tribe of monkeys lived in the king's pleasure garden. The monkeys played and chattered all day long, swinging from the branches of the trees and eating the fresh fruits and flowers.

One day the king's gardener thought, "There will soon be a big celebration in the city. If I can get the monkeys to do the simple task of watering for me, I can go to the celebration and enjoy myself along with everyone else. Surely the monkeys can do no harm by watering the trees." So the gardener went to the king of the monkeys to try to get his help.

The gardener began his request by pointing out to the monkey king the benefits he and his subjects enjoyed while living in the garden, where they could eat all the flowers, fruit, and young shoots they desired. The gardener ended by saying, "Today there is a great holiday in the city. I would like to go and enjoy the festivities. Will you water the young trees for me while I'm away?"

"Oh yes," said the monkey king eagerly.

The gardener gave the monkeys his waterskins and wooden watering pots to use. Then, saying, "Be sure that you do as you have promised," he left for the city.

The monkeys took the waterskins and watering pots and began running from tree to tree, sprinkling each in turn. As he watched the monkeys at their work, the king of the monkeys became worried that they would run out of water before they were done. It was a long way to the river to get more water, and so he devised a plan.

"We must not waste water," he said to his followers, "for when it is all gone it will be hard to get more." Then he carefully instructed his loyal subjects to first pull up each young tree and look at the size of the roots, then give plenty of water to those with deep roots but only a little to those with shallow roots.

"What a clever idea!" said the other monkeys, and they did as their leader told them, thinking only of how much water they were saving.

At this point a wise man entered the garden. Seeing the monkeys, he asked them why they pulled up tree after tree and then gave them various amounts of water.

"Because these are our king's commands," answered the monkeys. "We are pulling the trees up to see how big their roots are and giving them just enough water so that none is wasted."

Their reply moved the wise man to reflect how even when they desire to do good, those who have not developed wisdom often succeed only in doing harm. And he recited this verse to the monkeys:

"Knowledge crowns endeavor with success,
while ignorance turns us toward foolishness.
Witness the monkeys that tend the garden
     trees:
they unknowingly do harm even as they
     try to please."

With this rebuke to the king of the monkeys, the wise man left the pleasure garden.

THE TWO MERCHANTS

O nce upon a time a great leader of men was born into a merchant's family in Benares. When he grew up and became a merchant himself, he traveled across northern India with five hundred carts, journeying back and forth from east to west and from west to east. There was also another young merchant living in Benares, a foolish young man who lacked common sense.

One day the wise merchant loaded five hundred carts with costly wares from Benares. He was about to start out on his travels when he saw that the other young merchant had also loaded five hundred carts and was ready to begin a journey along the same road.

The wise merchant thought to himself, "If this foolish young merchant keeps me company all the way and the thousand carts travel along together, we will all be in danger. It will be difficult to get

51

wood, water, and food for the men or grass for the oxen. One of us must go on first."

So he sent for the other merchant and presented his idea to him. "The two of us cannot travel together safely," he said. "Would you rather go first or last?"

The foolish merchant thought, "There will be many advantages if I go first. The road will not be cut up; my oxen will have the pick of the grass; my men will have the pick of the herbs for curry; the water will be undisturbed; and lastly, I will fix my own price for the barter of my goods." So he replied, "I will go first, dear sir."

The wise merchant, on the other hand, saw many advantages in going last. "Those who go first will level the road where it is rough, while I will travel along the road they have already traveled," he thought. "Their oxen will have grazed off the coarse old grass, while mine will pasture on the sweet young growth which will spring up in its place. Where there is no water, the first caravan will have to dig to supply themselves, and we will drink at the wells they have dug." Accordingly, seeing all these advantages, he said to the other merchant, "Then you go on first, dear sir."

"Very well, I will," said the foolish merchant, and he yoked his carts and set out. Soon he had left human settlements behind him and came to the outskirts of the wilderness.

Now according to Indian legend, there are five kinds of wilderness: robber wilderness, wild-beast wilderness, dry desert, demon wilderness, and famine wilderness. In the robber wilderness the way is beset by thieves; in the wild-beast wilderness the way is beset by lions and other fierce animals; the dry desert has no water for drinking or bathing; in the demon wilderness the road is beset by goblins; and in the famine wilderness there are no roots or other food to be found. The wilderness traveled by our two merchants was both a dry desert wilderness and a demon wilderness.

The young merchant loaded huge water jars on his carts and filled them with water, then set out to cross the two hundred miles of desert that stretched before him. When his caravan reached the middle of the desert, the goblin who haunted it said to himself, "I will make these men throw away their jars of water, and when they are exhausted and weak, I will devour them all, leaving nothing but their bones."

Through his magical power the goblin conjured up a sumptuous carriage drawn by pure white young bulls. Accompanied by a retinue of a dozen goblins, he rode along to meet the merchant's caravan like a mighty lord in his carriage. His head was wreathed with blue lotuses and white waterlilies, his head and clothes were wet, and his carriage wheels were muddy.

His attendants also wore blue lotuses and white waterlilies wreathed in their wet hair. In their hands they carried bunches of white lotuses and chewed on the succulent stalks. Water gushed from the stalks, as if the lotuses had been plucked from nearby ponds and lakes.

The young merchant rode in front of his caravan. When the goblin saw him approaching, he drew his carriage off the road and greeted the merchant kindly, asking where he was going. The merchant also ordered his carriage to be drawn off the road to let the rest of the caravan pass while he spoke with the goblin.

"We are just on our way from Benares, sir," the merchant informed the seeming lord. "But I see you have lotuses and waterliles on your heads and in your hands; your people are chewing the tasty lotus stalks, and you are all muddy and dripping wet. Did it rain while you were on the road? Did you come upon pools covered with lotuses and waterlilies?"

The goblin exclaimed, "Rain, did you say? Why, see in the distance the dark green streak of the forest? From there on there is nothing but water all through the forest. It is always raining there. The pools are full, and on every side there are lakes covered with lotuses and waterlilies."

As the line of carts passed by, the goblin asked where they were going. "To such and such a place," was the reply.

"And what wares do you have in the cart?"

"Such and such."

"And what do you have in this last cart which seems to move as if it were heavily laden?"

"Oh, there's water in that."

"You did well to carry water with you. But there's no need for it now, since water is plentiful on ahead," advised the goblin. "So break the jars and throw the water away to make your travel easier." And he added, "Now continue on your way—you must be anxious to reach the cool forest pools." Then the goblin and his followers rode on to the goblin city where they lived.

So foolish was the young merchant that he took the goblin's advice and broke all his jars and poured the water on the sand. Then he ordered the carts, much lighter and faster now, to drive on.

They traveled all day, but they did not find even a drop of water. The men grew exhausted from thirst. At sunset they unyoked their carts and made camp, tying their oxen to the wheels. With no water for the oxen to drink, and no water for the men to cook their rice, the tired band sank down to the ground and went to sleep.

At midnight, the goblins came out of their city and killed the exhausted men and oxen. They devoured their flesh down to the bare bones and tossed the skeletons away, while leaving untouched the five hundred carts and their loads.

In Benares, the wise merchant, not knowing of the foolish merchant's fate, allowed six weeks to pass and then left the city with his five hundred carts. In due course his caravan came to the outskirts of the wilderness. Here he had the water jars filled with an ample supply of water.

Then he sounded the drum to gather his men together and spoke to them. "We must guard our water carefully. Let not even a palmful of water be used without my permission." Heeding his advice, his men followed him into the wilderness with their five hundred carts.

When they reached the middle of the wilderness, the goblin appeared on their path just as he had appeared to the foolish merchant. But as soon as the wise merchant became aware of the goblin, he thought, "There's no water here in this great dry wilderness, long known as the 'Waterless Desert'. This person with his red eyes and aggressive bearing casts no shadow. Very likely he will try to persuade me to throw away all my water, and then, when my men and I are exhausted, he will kill us and feed on our flesh. He will not succeed."

He shouted to the goblin, "Go away! We are men of business and do not throw away what we have until we see the source of more. When we do see more, you can be sure we will throw this water away and lighten our carts."

The goblin rode on a little way until he was out of sight and then returned to the demon city. When the goblin had gone, the merchant's men said to him, "Sir, we heard from those men that up ahead where you can see the dark green streak of the forest, it is always raining. They had lotuses on their heads and waterlilies in their hands and were eating the stalks. Water was streaming off their clothes and hair. Let us throw away our water so we can move on a little more quickly."

On hearing these words, the merchant ordered a halt and assembled all the men together. "Tell me," he said, "have any of you ever heard before today that there is a lake or pool in this wilderness?"

"No, sir," they replied. "It is known as 'the Waterless Desert'."

"We have just been told by some people that it is raining on ahead in the forest. Now how far does a rain wind carry?"

"About three miles, sir."

"Has anyone here seen the top of even a single storm-cloud?"

"No, sir."

"How far off can you see a flash of lightning?"

"Twelve or fifteen miles, sir."

"Has anyone here seen a flash of lightning?"

"No, sir."

"How far off can a man hear a clap of thunder?"

"Six or eight miles, sir."

"Has anyone here heard a clap of thunder?"

"No, sir."

"These are not men but goblins," said the merchant. "They will return to devour us when we are weak and faint with thirst if we throw our water away, as they suggest. The young merchant who went on before us was not resourceful, and I fear that he was fooled into throwing his water away. If this is so, we can expect to find his skeleton and his five hundred carts on the road ahead. Push ahead with all possible speed, without throwing away a drop of water."

Urging his men forward with these words, he proceeded on the way until they came to the five hundred carts standing just as they had been loaded and the skeletons of the men and oxen lying strewn about in every direction. He had his carts unyoked and arranged in a circle to form a strong camp and saw to it that both men and oxen had their supper early. The oxen were then made to lie down in the middle with the men around them, and he himself, along with the leading men of his band, stood on guard, sword in hand, throughout the night. Seeing the camp so well prepared, the goblins did not dare to attack.

At daybreak, after the oxen had been fed and everything else was done, the merchant replaced his own weak carts with stronger ones and substituted the most costly of the abandoned goods for the least costly of his own. Then he went on to his destination, where he bartered his stock for wares three times more valuable and came back to his own city without losing a single man.

Accepting the goblin's words without question, the foolish merchant and his men all lost their lives. The wise merchant, who respected what others had told him, observed carefully for himself and questioned what seemed too good to be true. As a result, he and his men returned safely and spent the rest of their lives in good deeds.

THE WHAT-FRUIT TREE

Once upon a time a wise leader was born into a merchant family. One day when he was grown up and had a trading caravan of five hundred wagons, he came to a place in the road that led to a great forest.

Halting at the outskirts, the wise leader summoned everyone in the caravan together and said: "Poison trees grow in this forest. Be careful not to taste any leaf, flower, or fruit without first consulting me." Everyone promised to be extremely careful, and the journey into the forest began without further delay.

Now just within the forest border stood a village, and just outside that village grew a what-fruit tree. The what-fruit tree resembled a mango tree exactly—in trunk, branch, leaf, flower, and fruit, not to mention taste and smell. The fruit hung from the tree's branches, within easy reach, enticing travelers to taste and eat. But, whether eaten ripe or unripe, the fruit was a deadly poison.

A few travelers with the caravan went on ahead of the carts. Coming to this tree, they took it to be a mango and greedily ate some of the fruit. But others said, "Let us ask our leader before we eat." Fruit in hand, they waited patiently by the tree until the merchant arrived. Perceiving that it was not a mango, the merchant said, "This is a what-fruit tree; don't touch its fruit."

Having stopped them from eating the poisonous fruit, the merchant turned to those who had already eaten. First he gave them a dose of a powerful medicine, and then he gave them four sweet foods to eat, so that they all recovered.

Before this, whenever caravans halted beneath this what-fruit tree, everyone had died from eating the poisonous fruit which they mistook for mangoes. Then people from the village had buried the bodies and taken the entire caravan—oxen, carts, and all of the merchant's wares.

On the day of our story, the villagers hurried to the tree at daybreak for their expected spoils. "We want the oxen," said some. "And we'll have the wagons," said others, while the rest claimed the wares as their share. But when they arrived breathless at the tree, they found everyone in the caravan alive and well!

"How did you know this was not a mango tree?" demanded the disappointed villagers.

"We didn't know," said the people of the caravan. "It was our leader who knew."

So the villagers went up to the leader and asked, "Man of wisdom, what did you do to find out that this tree was not a mango?"

"Two things told me," replied the wise merchant, reciting this stanza:

"When near a village stands a fruit-laden tree
not hard to climb, 'tis plain to me,
nor need I further proof to know—,
no wholesome fruit thereon can grow!"

Having taught the assembled multitude to temper greed with wisdom and compassion, he finished his journey in safety. Thus the wise merchant demonstrated how observation and clear thinking can moderate strong desires and protect us from danger.

THE KINGSHUK TREE
AND THE FOUR PRINCES

L ong ago in the city of Benares there ruled a powerful king who had four sons. One day when the princes were at school their teacher told them a story about the beautiful kingshuk tree that had dark red flowers in spring.

Since the palace garden had no kingshuks, none of the princes had ever seen the famous red blossoms. So they went to the driver of the royal chariot and said, "Sir, we have never seen a kingshuk tree. How we wish we could see one! Please, charioteer, would you take us to one?"

The charioteer replied, "Of course, my little princes!"

But instead of taking all four of them at the same time, he made four separate trips to the forest, so that each would have a chance to see the tree at a different time of year.

He made his first trip with the oldest son. It was the very beginning of springtime, and the sun came just a little earlier each morning to wake up the children and stayed just a little longer every evening to watch them play outside.

That morning the sun and his friend, the warm wind, had just given their first hugs to a lonely kingshuk tree after the long and bitter cold months of the north Indian winter. They put their kind arms around the sad, leafless tree and kissed her bare twigs and branches, whispering wakeup songs into her ears.

Tiny green glitters of leaves appeared all over the tree as she trembled at their tender touch and woke up. Yet so tiny were those green dots that they could hardly be seen. Like a newborn baby, the tree looked surprised by the world, and her dark and naked branches kept on shivering.

The prince's escort pointed to the tree and said, "There, Prince, take a look! That is a kingshuk tree."

A month went by. Then one day the charioteer approached the second prince. "My child, do you wish to spend the day at the forest today? The woods are beautiful now that spring is here. Maybe we could spot a kingshuk tree!"

The prince jumped up at the idea. Together they drove off to the forest. How the horses galloped! Their strong hooves struck the dusty path so mightily that a cloud of dust rose behind them and covered the trail at their back. In no time at all they were at the foot of the kingshuk tree.

Soft green leaves covered all the branches of the tree. They shone against the brilliant blue sky like emeralds set in a locket of sapphires. The dazzling tree looked down at the prince and smiled. As the hot wind blew through the leaves, they murmured, "Good morning, dear Prince!"

The prince looked at the tree and sighed. He did not know why but suddenly he felt very sad and lonely and yearned for a friend. Imagining that the tree wished to turn into a girl and be his friend, he returned to the palace with a heavy heart.

A few more weeks passed and the charioteer said to the third prince, "Come, my prince, let us take a ride to the forest. Do you still want to see a kingshuk tree?"

"Oh, yes! When can we leave?" said the prince.

"Right now, if you wish," replied the charioteer. So off they went, down the red dirt road, the wheels of the chariot rolling and roaring like a speeding, ferocious tiger. Soon they reached the spot by the woods where the kingshuk tree stood.

67

As the prince alighted from the chariot and looked up at the tree, he thought he was seeing the most beautiful sight in the world. What a majestic tree!

Every bough was decorated with luxurious blossoms of deep, dark red. The tree stooped low with the weight of the flowers. How carefully the wind touched the tips of her flowers! Any rough play would shake them to the ground.

The prince looked and looked and could not lift his eyes from the tree. He thought the kingshuk looked as beautiful in her red flowers as a bride on her wedding night, when she is draped in a gorgeous red silk sari.

As proud as a queen, the tree gazed deeply and steadily into the eyes of the prince, her eyes not downcast even for an instant. Like the magic moment of the wedding night when the bride and groom exchange glances for the very first time and join with each other by looking into one another's eyes, the prince and the tree stood still, without a stir, drinking the nectar of each other's eyes. Their eyes were loving and understanding, full of friendship and trust.

"Master, it is time for us to go," called the charioteer, who was getting ready to leave. "The sun is going down and it will soon be dark."

The prince walked slowly back to the chariot. As the chariot pulled away, the prince turned to look back at the kingshuk. Within minutes her red flowers were lost in the red clouds of dust and sunset.

Spring was over. The summer sun glared at the earth for long hours. One day the charioteer called the youngest prince to him.

"Little master, don't you wish to see the kingshuk tree like your brothers did?" said the charioteer.

"Oh yes I do, Charioteer! When are you taking me to the woods?" asked the boy eagerly.

The charioteer laughed. "Step inside the chariot and I am at your command," he said.

The heat of the day made the ride long and slow. The tired horses stopped to drink water and to rest under the shade. At dusk, after nibbling at some hay, they were ready to travel again. When the kingshuk tree came into view the sky and the dried fields had turned golden with the rays of the setting sun. "There, my little master, is your kingshuk. Take a look," said the charioteer.

The child looked up in reverence. The mature tree bore fruits on every little twig. The leaves were broad and dark green and looked strong and

69

tough. Hidden in her thick foliage and sturdy branches were nests where baby birds could be heard chirping.

The prince thought the tree looked like a mother, lost in her dreams about the futures of her children. Would all the tiny seeds of life sleeping in the warmth of the soft, juicy, fleshy fruits—still clinging to her for shelter and nourishment—survive in this rough world? Would they find their homes in the earth, strike roots there, sprout into seedlings, and grow into young kingshuks? Would they stand tall some day, encircling her, as though trying to give her protection and company in her old age?

As these thoughts moved through the prince's mind like autumn clouds, he suddenly felt that he wanted very much to go home and hug his mother.

"Charioteer! Please hurry! Take me home quickly—I want to see my mother. She must be looking out of the window for me, watching for signs of the chariot."

The charioteer smiled and raced home.

The heat of the summer had ended. It was the rainy season now, and showers poured down from the dark rain clouds like the blessings of a parent.

The lakes, ponds, and rivers were full, and the streets were flooded.

The schools were closed, and little children could be seen playing at their doorsteps with paper boats until their mothers called them inside for dinner.

On steaming hot rice their mothers poured melted butter and then briskly tossed pieces of fried fish on top; the fish was too hot to touch. For dessert there would be bowls of warm milk and bananas or sweet, thickened palm juice with condensed milk.

After dinner, with tired legs the children climbed up on the bed which always looked as vast as a paddy field sleeping in the moonlight. A dim lamp burned in a corner of the room. Huge shadows played on the walls. Grandma nestled in the bed with them to tell them the stories they had heard so many times that they knew them by heart.

Through the open door came the reassuring voices of the adults talking as they ate, making jokes, discussing business, complaining, or simply telling each other how the day had gone. The open windows let in gusts of monsoon winds, heavy with moisture and the fragrance of jasmines and tuberoses in full bloom.

Long before Grandma finished her story, the children had fallen fast asleep. Huddled close together, they were covered with a single, huge quilt that Grandma had stitched out of the old, worn-out saris of their mothers. The quilt still smelled like a mother's body, with its mixture of fragrances—food, scented hair-oil, soap, talcum powder. The children reached out for the quilt as sleep overcame them.

One rainy evening after dinner the four princes sat together and started talking about the kingshuk tree.

The oldest prince said, "I know what the kingshuk is like! It looks like a pillar that has been burned down and is about to be mended."

The second prince said, "I don't think you can be right, my dear brother. The kingshuk is as beautiful as a young girl waiting for her lover."

The third prince exclaimed, "I think both of you are mistaken. The kingshuk is neither dark nor green. It is red like the flames of fire."

"Dear brothers, all of you must have missed the real kingshuk tree," said the youngest prince. "For none of you spoke of the fruits hanging from the branches or the birds chirping from their nests in the tree."

In order to find out who had seen the real kingshuk tree, the four brothers went to the king and told him about their disagreements. "Father, can you tell us which one of us is correct?" the princes said.

"My sons," said the king, "there is no doubt that all four of you have seen the kingshuk tree. But each one of you has seen it only once, at one particular time of the year. None of you knows what it looks like at different times of the year. So none of you has really known the true kingshuk tree. To know something truly you must know how it appears at all times and not just at one time."

Each of us, having seen something with our own eyes, may think we know all there is to know about it. But because we may know only a part of the whole truth, it is important to listen to what others have to say about what they have seen and experienced. In this way our knowledge can grow and enrich everything we do.

THE MONSTER
OF THE LOTUS LAKE

Once upon a time in the city of Benares, a son named Peace was born to the king. When Peace was two years old and was beginning to run around on the palace grounds, a second son named Moon was born. But by the time Moon turned two and had started to run around, the queen died.

After some time, the king married again. He delighted in his new queen, who could always bring a smile to his face. When a son was born to her, the king was overjoyed.

The king named the child Sun, and in gratitude to the queen he said, "Beloved, I will grant you anything you wish for this child."

The queen replied, "There is nothing that I could wish for at this time. However, if and when I have a wish, I shall remind your lordship of your promise."

75

In time the princes grew from boyhood to manhood. The queen saw that the time was now right for her to remind the king of his promise to her. She proposed that the king take an oath to give the throne to her son after his death.

The astonished king replied, "But I cannot do injustice to my two older sons. They are as brave and pure of heart as the flames of a blazing fire. How can I deprive them of their right to the throne and give everything to your son?"

But the queen did not give up easily. Day and night she demanded that the king keep his promise. Fearing that the angry queen might attempt to harm her stepsons, the king called his sons aside. After explaining the situation, he said, "Go hide in the forest, my sons, until I die. When you hear of my death, return and wear the crown. By law, the throne belongs to the eldest son."

So saying, he kissed his sons goodbye and retired to his room, lamenting.

After saluting their father, the two brothers set out from the palace with great sadness. Sun, the youngest prince, was playing in the yard. He was surprised to see Peace and Moon leaving the palace on foot, dressed as common people.

When he learned why they were leaving, he became very sad. Not wishing to stay behind and enjoy kingship while his brothers had to give up what rightfully belonged to them, he took a vow to follow them wherever they went and to share their hardships. And so the three brothers left the palace together.

After crossing many plains and rivers, the princes finally reached the Himalayan Mountains. It was midday, and the sun was hot. The three tired princes sat down in the shade of a tree.

After resting a while, Peace said to Moon, "Dear brother, I feel a fresh breeze—I think there is a lake nearby. Would you go find it? Take a good dip in the cool waters, and have a long refreshing drink. When you are ready to return, pluck a lotus leaf, make a bowl out of it, and bring back some water for us to drink."

The princes did not know that the nearby lake belonged to Kuber, the God of Wealth, nor did they know that Kuber had given the lake to a monster to live in. Kuber had made a deal with the monster, saying, "If someone who does not know right and wrong enters my lake, you may eat that person. However, you cannot touch those who remain on the shore."

The monster always posed the same question to anyone who entered the lake: "What is right and what is wrong?" The monster gobbled up anyone who could not answer correctly, although secretly he longed to hear the true answer.

Moon, not knowing this, jumped into the lake quite happily. The monster instantly raised its head above the waters and grabbed him.

"Brother, do you know what is right and what is wrong?"

"Certainly," said Moon. "Actions that are sun-like or moonlike are right. The rest are wrong."

"Your answer is not fully correct, so I will keep you captive in my prison for now." He dragged Moon under the waters and imprisoned him in a castle.

Noticing that Moon was late in returning, Peace sent Sun to look for him. The sparkling waters of the lake and the huge lotuses swaying in the mild waves tempted the young prince.

"Let me refresh myself first," he thought. "Then I will look for Moon. He must be in the woods looking for fruit."

Sun splashed into that beautiful lotus-filled lake. The monster immediately emerged from the waters.

"Can you tell the difference between right and wrong?" inquired the monster.

"Of course," said Sun. "An action is right when it is done after giving due thought to all that is happening in each of the four directions. Thoughtless actions, done in haste, tend to be wrong."

"Not completely correct!" gloated the monster. The fate of Sun was the same as that of Moon. The monster took him to the fortress under the lake and held him captive there.

When hours had passed and neither of the brothers had returned, Peace began to fear for their safety. Hurriedly he set out to look for them. Following their footsteps, he reached the lake. When he saw that all of the footsteps led into the water and none came out of it, he knew that both brothers had ended up in the lake.

But how could they drown? Sun and Moon both knew how to swim. He began to suspect some foul play. Sword in hand, he started to walk cautiously around the lake.

The monster saw that Peace kept to the shore. In order to tempt him to step down into the lake, the monster magically assumed the figure of a hunter and appeared before Peace.

"Brother," he said, "you look tired. You must have traveled a long way. Why don't you bathe in this beautiful lake? Wade into the water and have a drink. The lotuses are sweet enough to eat. After you enjoy them, you can make lotus garlands to wear that will cool you down."

Peace's suspicions were aroused. Why was this stranger so insistent upon his entering the lake? Besides, Peace sensed that the hunter was somehow not quite like a normal human being.

"I am looking for my two brothers. Do you have anything to do with their disappearance?"

Seeing that Peace could not be easily tricked, the monster decided to be honest. He said, "Yes, I am holding them as my prisoners."

"But why?"

"Because they entered the lake without being able to correctly tell right from wrong," said the monster.

"So you want to know what it is that makes actions right?"

"Yes, that is what I want to know."

"Well, I can tell you that if you will release at least one of my brothers."

"I will do it," was the monster's reply.

"I will tell you what I know. But I am so thirsty and tired that I can hardly speak," Peace said.

By this time the monster's curiosity to know what made actions right and wrong had become very strong. He immediately agreed to help Peace. He fetched water from the lake and let him have a bath on the shore. He brought him food and drink and put lotus garlands around Peace's neck. He quickly set up a tent and placed a bed inside it. When Peace reclined on the bed, the monster sat down at his feet, as a proper student does.

Satisfied with the respectful treatment he had received, Peace felt ready to share his knowledge of right and wrong with the monster. So he spoke:

"The one whose mind is not agitated
    with anger,
the one who holds on to truth without fear,
the one who constantly strives to be free
of hateful thoughts and thoughts of revenge,
is the compassionate, the fearless, and the
    free one.
His actions are right."

These words totally satisfied the monster. He bowed his head in reverence and said: "You are a wise man. I can return only one life by our contract, but as a special favor, I will spare your life too. So, tell me, which one of your brothers do you desire me to set free?"

"Bring my youngest brother Sun," said Peace.

81

"I am disappointed," the monster said. "You have knowledge of right and wrong, but you do not act rightly. It is customary to treat the older one with more respect, for he has more rights. Why do you want to save the life of your younger brother while the older one is still in danger? What will people say?"

"Dear monster," said Peace, "not only do I know right from wrong, but I also try to do the right thing. Although age makes people wise and so more worthy of respect, it does not always give them more rights. Some rights belong to all, young or old. Sometimes the young may have more claim because they need more protection.

"As for Sun, not only is he the youngest, needing most help, but also he happens to be my stepmother's son. He followed us into exile out of his own choice because he loved us so much, even more than the future crown. How can we abandon someone who did not abandon us and loves us more than he loves himself? Not once has he mentioned home in all these years with us.

"It is not right to do something out of fear of what others might say. I do what appears right to me until someone can convince me that it is wrong. Moreover, if I say that a monster has eaten my stepbrother, no one will believe me. They will think I have killed him to take the throne from him. None of the people will support me then. Therefore, if you will return only one of my brothers, I beg of you again to return Sun to me."

The monster was delighted at the kind, just, and wise thoughts of Peace. To show his gratitude to his teacher for giving him such valuable knowledge, he released both brothers from the prison.

From that day on, the three brothers and the monster became the best of friends. The monster looked after the brothers for as long as they lived in the forest. Then one night, by studying the stars, Peace saw that their father, the king, had passed away. In keeping with his promise to his father, he returned to the palace with Sun and Moon.

The people gave the crown to Peace. Moon became Viceroy for the outer territories, and Sun was appointed his Commander-in-Chief. The new king did not forget his old friend, the monster. He built for him a beautiful palace by a lovely lake, close to the royal gardens. Every day he sent him the best of food and flowers and incense.

No one knows what happened to the stepmother who had forced the king to send Peace and Moon to the forest because she wanted her own son to be king. But we can be sure that Peace, guided by compassion, did not harm her in any way.

PRINCE SAMVARA AND
THE NINETY-NINE PRINCES

Once upon a time in Benares there lived a Prince named Samvara, the youngest of the king's one hundred sons. The king placed each of his sons with a different courtier and instructed the courtiers to give the princes a fitting education. The courtier who instructed Prince Samvara was a man of wisdom and great learning. He was like a father to the king's son.

After each of the sons was educated, the courtier who had instructed him brought him to see the king. The king gave each prince a province to govern and bid him farewell.

When Prince Samvara had been perfected in all learning, he asked his wise teacher, "Dear friend and guide, if my father sends me to a province, what am I to do?"

"My son," replied the courtier, "when a province is offered you, you should refuse it and say, 'My lord, I am the youngest of all. If I go too, there will be no one at your feet. I will remain where I am, at your feet.'"

One day, when Prince Samvara had saluted his father and was standing by his side, the king asked him, "Well, my son, have you finished your learning?"

"Yes, my lord."

"Then choose a province."

"My lord, if I go too, there will be no one at your feet. Let me remain here and in no other place!"

The king was pleased and consented.

After that Prince Samvara remained in the palace at the king's feet. And again, he asked the courtier, "What else am I to do, honored elder?"

"Ask the king," the courtier answered, "for some old park."

The prince agreed and asked his father for a park. Because of the park's abundant natural wealth, the prince made friends with the most powerful men in the city, offering them all kinds of fruit and flowers.

Again he asked his guardian what to do. "Ask the king's leave, my son," said the wise one, "to distribute alms for the poor and worthy within the city." So he did, and without neglecting even a single person, he distributed food and money within the city.

Again he asked the wise courtier's advice, and after soliciting the king's consent, he distributed food within the palace to the servants, the horses, and the army, forgetting no one. When messengers came from foreign countries he found them a place to stay and made sure their needs were met. He also took care of the needs of merchants, making all the necessary arrangements himself.

Thus, following the advice of his wise guardian, he made friends with everybody, rich and poor, those in the household and those outside, the people in the city, the subjects of the kingdom as well as outsiders, binding them to him by his winsomeness as if it were a band of iron. To all of them he was dear and beloved.

When in due time the king lay on his deathbed, the courtiers asked him, "When you are dead, my lord, to whom shall we give the White Umbrella, the great symbol of your kingship?"

"Friends," he said, "all my sons have a right to the White Umbrella. But you may give it to the one who pleases your heart."

After the king's death, when the funeral ceremonies had been performed, all of the courtiers gathered together on the seventh day and said, "Our king bade us give the Umbrella of Kingship to the prince who pleases our heart. The one who our heart desires is Prince Samvara." Over Prince Samvara, escorted by his kinsmen, they therefore lifted up the White Umbrella with its festoons of gold.

The other ninety-nine princes heard that their father was dead and that the Umbrella had been lifted up over Samvara.

"But he is the youngest of all," they said. "The Umbrella does not belong to him. Let us raise the Umbrella over the eldest of us all." They joined forces and sent a letter to Samvara, bidding him resign the Umbrella or fight. Then they surrounded the city.

The new king told this news to his wise guardian and asked for his advice. He answered, "Great King, you must not fight with your brothers. Divide the treasure belonging to your father into a hundred portions, and send ninety-nine of them to your brothers with this message: 'Accept this share of your father's treasure, for fight with you I will not.'" So he did.

Then the eldest of all the brothers, Prince Uposatha, summoned the rest together and said to them, "Friends, there is no one able to overcome this king. Although our youngest brother has been our enemy, he does not remain so—he sends us his wealth and refuses to fight with us. Now we cannot all lift up the Umbrella at the same moment. Let us uplift it over one only, and let him alone be king. When we see the king, we will hand over the royal treasure to him and return to our provinces."

All the princes halted the siege of the city and then entered it, enemies no longer. The king instructed his courtiers to welcome them and sent them to meet the princes. With a great following and in all humility toward the great king Samvara, the princes entered on foot, mounted the steps of the palace, and sat down beneath the king.

King Samvara was seated under the White Umbrella upon a throne. Great magnificence and pomp seemed natural to him; whatever he looked upon trembled and quaked. Prince Uposatha, the eldest born, seeing the magnificence of the mighty King Samvara, thought, "Our father, I think, knew that Prince Samvara would be king after his decease, and he therefore gave us provinces and gave him none." Addressing the king, he spoke these words:

"Our father surely knew very well what kind of nature you have, mighty monarch, and for this reason he gave his ninety-nine sons their own provinces, but gave you, the youngest, none.

Samvara, tell us about your power. Why is it that your older brothers do not make war against you in order to gain the kingship?"

King Samvara then explained his own character: "I have never, Prince and brother, withheld from great wise men such as the Great Sage who instructed me, what is due to them. I am always ready to pay them honor. I do not envy anyone and wish to learn all ways of being in the world that are right and proper—so I have listened to each good teaching that wise sages delight in.

"I not only listen but follow the instruction of the sages. My heart is drawn to good intentions, and I do not turn away from good counsel, even if the advice does not seem easy.

"The troops of the city—the charioteers, the soldiers who ride the elephants, the guards, the royal infantry—received every penny that was their fee. I took no part of their earnings.

"Great noblemen and women and wise counselors from all over the world attend my court. They return to their lands and tell about the abundant food, water, and wine of Benares. Thus the merchants prosper and are welcome in many realms. I take care to protect them.

"Now, Uposatha, eldest brother, you know of my life and rule."

After hearing this account of King Samvara's character and practices, Prince Uposatha said to him, "You are so wise and prudent, Samvara, that all your brothers shall bless you. Be elevated as king above us, your kin, and rule in righteousness. Your brethren will gladly defend your treasure, and you shall be as safe from your foes as Indra, lord of the gods, is from his greatest enemy."

King Samvara gave great honor to all his brothers. They remained with him a month and a half. Then they said to him, "Great King, we wish to go and see if there are any bandits afoot in our provinces. May you rule in all happiness!"

They departed, each to his province. And for the rest of his life the king lived by the precepts of generosity and nonviolence which he had learned from his teacher, the Great Sage.

THE GOLDEN BOWL

O nce upon a time a wise merchant who traded pots and pans in the ancient kingdom of Seri became known as 'the Serivan'. In the same kingdom there was a greedy fellow who traded the same wares. He too was called 'the Serivan'.

One day both these tradesmen crossed the Telavaha River and entered the city of Andhapura. Dividing up the streets between them, the two potsellers set about hawking their wares, each in their section of the city.

In that city lived a family who had once been rich merchants but had lost all their sons and brothers as well as all their wealth. The sole survivors were a girl and her grandmother who made their living by working as servants. In their house was a golden bowl out of which the great merchant, the head of the family, had always eaten in the old days. Having been unused for many years, it had been thrown among the pots and pans and was covered with dirt, so that the two women did not know it was made of gold.

Making his rounds, the greedy hawker came to the door of their house. "Waterpots for sale! Waterpots for sale!" he called.

Hearing him, the girl said to her grandmother, "Oh grandmother, please buy me a trinket."

"We're very poor, my dear," the grandmother said. "What can we offer in exchange?"

"Why here's this bowl that is no good to us," replied the girl. "Let's exchange it for a trinket."

The old woman had the hawker brought in and gave him a seat. Then she gave him the bowl, saying, "Take this, sir, and be so good as to give this young girl something in exchange."

The hawker took the bowl in his hands, turned it over, and suspecting it was gold, scratched a line on the back of it with a needle. Seeing for certain that it was gold, he thought, "I can get this bowl for nothing—without giving them anything at all in exchange!" He said to the women, "What value is this? Why it isn't even worth a dime!" He threw the bowl on the ground, rose up from his seat, and left the house.

The two hawkers had an agreement that when one of them was finished with a street, the other could also try his wares there. So soon the wise merchant went to that same street and appeared at the door of the house, crying, "Waterpots for sale!" Once again the young girl asked her grandmother to buy her a little gift.

"My dear," replied the grandmother, "the first hawker threw our bowl on the ground and left the house. What do we have to offer now?"

"That hawker was a harsh-spoken man, dear grandmother, while this one looks like a nice man who speaks kindly," said the girl. "Very likely he will take the bowl."

"Call him in then," said the grandmother.

So the hawker came into the house, and they gave him a seat and put the bowl into his hands. Seeing that the bowl was gold, he said, "Madam, this bowl is worth a hundred thousand pieces. I don't have wares of that much value with me."

"Sir, the first hawker who came here said it wasn't worth even a dime," the grandmother said. "He threw it to the ground and went away. It must have been the merit of your own goodness that has turned the bowl into gold. Take it; give us something for it, and go on your way."

At that time the hawker had with him five hundred pieces of money and a stock worth that much again. He gave all of this to the girl and her grandmother, saying, "Let me keep my scales, my bag, and eight pieces of money." With their consent he took these with him and departed, going as quickly as he could to the riverside. There he gave his eight coins to the boatman and jumped into the boat.

Meanwhile the greedy hawker came back to the house and asked the grandmother to bring out the bowl, saying he would give them something for it. But the old woman flew at him with these words, "You claimed that our golden bowl—which is worth a hundred thousand pieces—was not worth even a dime. But an upright merchant—your master, I take it—gave us a thousand pieces for it and took it away."

"He has robbed me of a golden bowl worth a full hundred thousand pieces!" exclaimed the greedy hawker. "He has caused me a terrible loss."

Overcome with intense anger, he lost control of himself. He threw his money and his goods at the door of the house; he tore off his upper garments and his undershirt. Armed with the beam of his scales as a club, he tracked the wise hawker down to the riverside.

Finding that the wise hawker was already crossing the river, he shouted to the boatman to turn back. But the wise hawker told the boatman not to return. As the greedy hawker stood there gazing furiously at the retreating boat and its passenger, he was seized with such intense longing that his heart cracked like sun-dried mud at the bottom of a dry creek. Through the hatred that filled his heart to bursting, he expired right then and there.

Seeing such suffering, the wise hawker felt great compassion for his fellow merchant and vowed to live a life completely free of greed and anger from that day forth.

THE LION'S SKIN

L ong ago there once lived a traveling merchant who used a donkey to carry his load of merchandise from town to town. When the day's work was done, the merchant let his donkey loose in the neighboring farmlands. But first he would cover it with a lion's skin, so people would mistake it for a lion. Then the donkey would freely roam around the paddy and oat fields eating the standing crops. When it grew dark, the donkey would find its way back to the merchant and settle down for the night.

This trick worked, for the people who guarded the fields were afraid to go near a lion. So the merchant continued to sell to the townspeople during the day and trick them every evening.

One morning the merchant decided that both he and his donkey would have a good breakfast before setting out for work. Just before he sat

99

down to prepare his breakfast he covered the donkey with the lion's skin and let it wander off into the oat fields nearby, even though it was broad daylight and the sun was shining brightly.

When the field guards saw the lion roaming around in the fields, they became excited and said to one another, "Look! The lion has come! The farmers are awake now and will soon be coming out into the fields. Let us go and tell them that the lion is here and is eating their crops! Maybe we can band together and drive the lion away."

They went inside the village and called the farmers to report what they had seen. The farmers were just getting ready to go to work. They quickly collected whatever weapons and tools they could find and ran towards the fields, blowing their conchshells and beating their drums.

When they reached the field where the donkey was grazing, they raised a big hullabaloo to scare the animal away. They yelled loudly and waved their arms while beating the drums and sounding the conchshells in a loud crescendo. "Away, lion, go away! Away!" they shouted, jumping up and down and knocking their weapons together to make a loud noise.

Hearing the clamor and seeing the farmers advancing toward him, the donkey became frightened. As the farmers drew nearer, he became so terrified he could not move or make a sound. Not until the farmers were so close they could see his legs under the lion's skin did the donkey open his mouth and begin to bray. Hearing the braying, the farmers suddenly realized that the animal was not a lion but a donkey!

The farmers became so angry at the donkey and its master that they drove them both out of the village that very day. When their neighbors realized that the merchant had also cheated them by his trickery, they drove both the merchant and his donkey out of their towns and villages as well. As a result of his dishonesty, the merchant lost both his reputation and his livelihood.

THE MONKEY
AND THE PEAS

Once upon a time a man renowned for his wisdom became the chief counselor and trusted friend of the king of Benares, advising the king on both spiritual and political matters. One day, after many years of peace, fighting broke out among the troops who guarded the borders, and loyal soldiers sent a letter to their king requesting his help in putting down the rebellion.

Now the border was far away. The roads wound through steep hills and the journey there was hazardous even in good weather. The monsoon season had already begun. Dark clouds were sweeping through the sky, rain was coming down in torrents, and wind had driven animals and people alike into shelter. The roads were soft and muddy and the hillsides were vulnerable to land-slides. Nevertheless, the king decided to go to the border to end the rebellion. He gathered his army and set out on the road.

At the end of the first day's march, the troops set up camp in one of the king's parks. After the king sat down to rest, the counselor came before him, ready to assist him in any way possible.

At that very moment, a servant poured steamed peas into a trough for the horses to eat. Seeing this, one of the monkeys that lived in the park jumped down from a tree overhead, filled his mouth and hands with peas, then jumped up again. Sitting in the tree, he began to eat.

As he ate, one pea fell from his hand to the ground. Scrambling to catch the lost pea, the monkey dropped all the peas from his hands and mouth. He then climbed down from the tree to look for his lost pea. He looked under the tree and all around it, but he could not find that pea. So he climbed up his tree again and sat still, glumly looking like someone who had lost a lot of money.

The king observed what the monkey had done and pointed it out to the counselor. "Friend, what do you think of that?" he asked.

The counselor answered, "King, this is what fools of little wit are used to doing; they spend a dollar to get a penny," and he recited this verse:

"A foolish monkey, living in the trees,
both his hands chock full of peas,
loses them all to look for one:

There is no wisdom, Sire, in what
he's done."

Then the counselor came nearer to the king and, addressing him again, recited a second verse:

"Such are we, O mighty monarch,
such all those who greedy be,
losing much to gain a little,
like the monkey and the pea."

On hearing this, the king thought of his kingdom rich in grain and jewels and of his people whom he was leaving unprotected. He suddenly realized his folly in undertaking a dangerous journey to maintain control of a small border province. Resolving not to make the same mistake as the monkey, he turned around and went straight back to Benares without wasting another moment.

The rebels, who had heard that the king had set forth from his capital to vanquish his enemies, disbanded and went away from the borders, fearing the king's wrath. Thus the king, mindful of what was most important, was able to protect the whole of his kingdom. Thereafter he ruled with greater wisdom, always remembering the lesson the greedy monkey had taught him.

THE TURTLE
AND THE SWANS

Many years ago, in a crystal clear lake at the foot of the huge, snowcapped Himalayan Mountains, there lived a turtle. Two white swans who came to the lake regularly in search of food often met the turtle, and in time the swans and the turtle became good friends.

One day the swans said to the turtle, "Dear friend, our home is by the golden cave in Chitrakut Peak, famous for its beauty. We would like to show you this pretty place. Do you want to come with us?"

The turtle replied, "But how will I go there? I cannot fly, and I walk very slowly."

"We can take you there," said the swans. "But you must promise us one thing."

"What is that?" asked the turtle.

107

"You must promise not to open your mouth or speak to anybody on the way," said the swans.

"Oh, that's no problem! I can keep my mouth shut!" the turtle replied.

The swans were delighted. "So, let us go off to the mountains!" said all three together.

Then the swans picked up a stick and gave it to the turtle. They instructed him, "All you have to do is to hold onto the middle part of the stick with your mouth while we hold the two ends." Then off they all flew, soaring across the sky.

As they flew over a village, some boys playing in the streets saw them and shouted excitedly, "Look! A turtle! The swans are carrying a turtle! Come, everybody! Look, look, a turtle in the sky!" They yelled and jumped up and down and started to chase the flying party.

The crowd of boys made the turtle very angry. "What is it to you, eternal pranksters? If I fly with my friends, how does that concern you? Are you up to your old tricks again? How I hate boys!" thought the turtle angrily, unable to open its mouth to speak.

Soon they reached the city of Benares, where they flew over the king's palace. The king's helpers were working down below in the courtyard. One of them looked up and spotted the flying turtle.

He called out to everybody else, and soon everyone was making terrible noises at the strange sight. The king's chef came out of the kitchen and joked, "What a fat turtle! I wish it would fall! What a splendid dinner it would make!"

At this the turtle could hold himself back no longer. He forgot his promise not to open his mouth. He wanted to shout out, "Eat the coal that burns in your stove!" But before he could say anything, down he came, falling to his death with a tremendous crash right in the middle of the courtyard. The swans flew away back home, sad to have lost their friend.

When the turtle's pride got the better of him, he forgot that it is often wiser to keep silent than to respond to foolish comments. His anger overcame his reason and he lost his life.

THE WOODCUTTER KING

Once upon a time, the king of Kosala was strolling in one of the royal gardens that lay outside the city. As he walked along, picking flowers and fruits, he came across a young woman humming a tune while she gathered dry twigs and sticks from the ground.

The more he watched her, the more deeply he was attracted to her. She moved with such beauty and grace that he could not let her out of his sight. When she spoke, her voice had a lilting music which soothed and calmed his restless spirit.

Day after day the king returned to the garden to see the young woman. He adorned her with garlands of flowers and built himself a sheltered bower in the garden so that he could be near her. Gradually he won her affection until one day she offered him garlands of flowers and entered his bower to live with him.

111

After they had spent a few happy months to-gether, the young woman was with child. Knowing this, the king gave her his signet ring and said, "Keep this ring in a safe place; my name and seal will give the child the right to call me father. Once the child is born, bring the baby to me. Be sure to bring this signet ring with you, for this is the proof of our union."

Shortly afterwards the king was called away to his duties. In due time the woman had a baby boy. She loved the baby with all her heart, but she did not understand why the king had left her behind to bear the child alone, or why he did not visit her or send any messengers to seek news of her. She loved the king and did not want to shame him or cause him any embarrassment, so she decided to raise her son by herself. Although she was poor and had to work for a living, she did not sell the king's ring for money to raise the child.

Months and years passed. The young mother gathered and chopped wood to support herself and her little son. Under her eyes, at times joyous, at times full of sorrow, he learned to smile, turn on his bed, sit up, and then crawl.

He would crawl under the table and turn all the pots and pans upside down. He would crawl into the backyard, watch the ants, and laugh at the birds as they hopped here and there pecking at the vegetables. Digging holes in the earth with his tiny fingers, he would laugh and play, scattering handfuls of dirt everywhere.

Then he learned to walk, setting his mother's arms free, but imprisoning her eyes, for her eyes had to follow him wherever he ran. Soon the boy was old enough to go outside and play with other children his age. Sometimes he was teased and nicknamed 'The No-Father Boy' because he had no father at home.

One day, feeling hurt, he asked his mother, "Mama, who is my father?"

"The king is your father, my child," she replied.

"But what is the proof, Mama?"

Then the mother showed him the signet ring the king had given her. After that day the boy began to ask his mother again and again to take him to his father. He was impatient to meet his father, to see how he looked and learn everything about him.

The mother realized that the boy was determined to find his father. So one morning she took the signet ring and set out on the road that led to the palace with her son.

Upon reaching the palace gate she showed the ring to the guards. Seeing the king's name and seal on the ring, the guards did not question her but brought her straight to the king. She proceeded to the throne where the king sat.

After bowing to the king she pointed to the boy and said, "My lord, here is your son."

The king knew her as soon as he saw her. But he did not acknowledge her. He felt extremely embarrassed in front of a courtful of people who knew nothing about the woman and his life with her. Pretending innocence, he said, "Nonsense! I have no son by you!"

Then the woman took out the ring and showed it to the king.

"This is not my ring," said the king. "This ring is a fake."

The woman exclaimed, "Only the gods witnessed our union. Will no one else speak for me?" As she stood alone before the king and his assembled court, she cried out to the very air to be her witness: "I will lift my son up into the air. If he is truly the son of this king, he will remain safely in midair. If he is not, then he will fall to the ground."

Saying this, the woman lifted the boy up into the air and dropped her arms to her sides. Then the most amazing of all things happened. Instead of falling to the ground, the boy remained comfortably suspended in the air. He called out to his father and said,

"Father, I am truly your son. Do not turn me away. You are the king of this vast land. Your palace is large and you give food and shelter to many people. My mother is poor and has worked hard to raise me; it will not trouble you to find a place for me and my mother in your house."

The king was moved. He stretched out his arms and said, "Come, my son. From this day forward you shall live with me. You and your mother shall have everything your hearts desire."

Seeing the king overcome with affection, the crowd clamored with raised hands, each person seeking to take the prince in his arms first. But the boy descended right onto the king's lap and laid his head on the king's shoulder. The king rose and greeted the boy's mother as his wife. He took them both inside the palace.

After spending many happy years with his family, the king died. Then the prince became king and wore the crown. But he never forgot that he was born of a poor woman who once labored in sorrow to be able to feed and clothe him. To show respect to his mother's toil and to honor her family's trade, he called himself 'The Woodcutter King'.

THE SERPENT
AND HIS JEWEL

Once upon a time the king of Benares had a very rich and famous teacher at his court. The teacher had two sons whom he loved dearly. But alas, the boys were barely out of school when they lost both their parents.

The loss left the two brothers in a state of shock. They decided to leave the city and travel for several months. They came to a beautiful spot by the Ganges River where they stayed for a while, each building a little hut out of twigs, branches, and leaves. The older brother lived in a hut up the bank, while the younger brother built his hut down the bank.

One day, soon after the boys' arrival, the king of the serpents came out of the waters of the Ganges to take a stroll on the riverbank. His palace under the river was very close to the place where the brothers had made their huts. As he was passing by the younger brother's hut, he saw the young man working in his garden. "What a hardworking and noble young man!" the serpent king thought. "Maybe we could be friends."

The serpent king did not want to frighten the young man away by appearing before him as a snake. Using his magic, he cast a spell that made him look like another young man. Then he went up to the prince and made his acquaintance.

They talked for a long time about all the things in the world, and then in the evening the serpent king left. The next day he came to see the boy again. He began to visit the younger brother every day, and the two became very close friends.

One day the serpent king thought, "Now that my friend knows me, he will not be afraid to see that I am really a snake. I think he will still love me as before."

So that day, just before leaving his friend, the serpent king assumed his real form. What a majestic snake he was! How tall he stood! On his hood glowed the famous jewel that adorns all serpent kings. It glowed like the peacock's neck, dark green gleaming from deep within midnight blue. Like the sky of daybreak it sent out its lovely rays of light—orange, rosy pink, and light yellow blending together in radiant splendor!

118

Although he tried not to show it, the boy became very frightened when he saw his friend turn into a snake. Each day the serpent king would come, and the two friends would talk and laugh all day long. Then at sundown, the serpent would change his form from that of a boy to that of a snake, embrace his friend, and depart for his palace under the river.

When the serpent king hugged him, the boy held his breath, trying to hide his fear. During the night he could not sleep. He was so afraid of the snake that he lost his appetite. For one week he did not eat well and grew thin and pale.

Finally, the boy went to visit his older brother. His brother was surprised to see him looking so thin.

"What has happened to you? Have you been sick?" the older brother asked.

"No, I have not been sick. But my mind is terribly troubled."

The boy told his story to his brother. The older brother listened and then said, "Are you so afraid of the snake that you do not want to see him any more?"

"Yes, I am too afraid," said the younger brother.

"Then do as I say. The snake has a precious jewel that gives him his magical powers. Tomorrow, just before the snake takes his leave, ask him to give you his jewel. If the snake returns the following day, don't let him in right away. Stop him at the front door and ask for the jewel. Most likely, the snake will want to go home instead of staying with you.

"On the third day, wait for your friend on the riverbank. As soon as you see him raising his head from the waters, ask for the jewel. I am sure you will not see him any more." The younger brother promised to follow these instructions and went back to his hut.

For the next three days the boy asked the snake for his jewel, just as his brother had advised. Although the serpent king loved his friend very much, he did not want to part with his jewel. He could not even imagine being without his precious jewel, the source of his power, beauty, and magic.

The serpent king grew very sad and thought to himself, "All my friend wants is my jewel. He does not love me anymore." He sighed and went back to his palace under the Ganges and did not come back again.

But the boy did not feel happy all alone in his hut. He began to think about the snake's magical jewel until he could think about nothing else.

In the past he had been so frightened of the snake that he had hardly noticed the jewel. But now, thoughts of the jewel filled his mind, and he dreamed of it day and night. He forgot to eat, drink, or sleep. He even forgot to visit his brother to tell him what had happened.

Soon his brother became anxious. He came down to see for himself if his brother was all right. He was shocked to see him as withered as a long-dead butterfly.

"What troubles you, brother? Did the serpent not stop coming?"

"Oh yes, he does not come any more."

"Then what is still bothering you?"

"I am bothered because the snake will not come."

"I thought you did not want to see him."

"I do not want to see him. I want his jewel."

"But my dear brother, the serpent will never give you his jewel unless you can show him that you care for him more than for his jewel. The more you ask for the jewel the more you will frighten him away. Love him as he loves you and he will share his jewel with you." Saying this, the older brother went away.

The boy started to think. Perhaps what his brother said was true! He made up his mind to try not to be afraid of the snake. He walked down to the river and called, "Friend! Please come out!"

When the serpent king heard the boy's voice he forgot his sad thoughts and raised his head out of the water.

"Did you call me, my friend?" said the snake.

"Yes, I did. Do you want to come to my hut and talk with me?"

"Yes, I would like that."

When the snake came up the boy tried to embrace him. His heart was still shaking with fear but he managed to quiet it. First he touched the snake with one hand, then with the other. The snake's skin felt smooth and cool. Then he looked into the snake's eyes. There he saw the love the snake had for him. His fear left him, and he hugged the serpent king.

The serpent king smiled and shook his head. The jewel fell down from his hood and lay at the boy's feet. The boy smiled too and picked up the beautiful shining jewel.

All day long he held the jewel and at sunset, when it was time for the serpent to return home, he put the jewel back on the serpent's head and said, "Good night, friend!"

"Good night," said the king of the serpents, and then he vanished into the darkness. For the rest of their lives they shared their friendship like a jewel, and their friendship became more precious and magical than they ever dreamed was possible.

THE LION
AND THE JACKAL

Once upon a time, a great-spirited lion was living in a cave in the hills. One day he came out from his lair and looked towards the foot of the mountain. All around the foot of the mountain stretched a great body of water.

Soft green grass grew on the thick mud that lay at the banks of the water, and over this mud ran rabbits and deer and other lightfooted creatures that ate the grass. On this day, as usual, there was a deer grazing on the grass.

"I'll have that deer!" thought the lion, and with a leap he sprang from the hillside towards the deer. The agile deer quickly scampered away, bellowing. But the lion could not stop his lunge; he fell down onto the mud, and his feet sank deeper and deeper until he could not possibly get himself out. There he remained for seven days, his feet fixed like four posts, with nothing to eat.

A jackal, hunting for food, happened to see the lion and started to run away in terror. But the lion called out to him.

"Jackal, don't run away—here I am, caught in the mud. Please save me!"

The jackal came up closer to him. "I could pull you out," he said, "but I am very afraid that once you are out you might eat me."

"Don't be afraid," said the lion. "I won't eat you. Certainly not, in fact I'll do you a great service in return for your kindness. Please, I will surely starve here without your help."

The jackal, accepting this promise, worked the mud away from the lion's four feet. He worked the holes that bound the lion's feet further towards the water, so the water could run in and soften the mud. Then he got underneath the lion. "Now, sir, one great effort together!" the jackal said, making a loud grunt and striking the lion's belly with his head. The lion strained every nerve and scrambled out of the mud onto dry land.

After a moment's rest, he plunged into the lake and scoured the mud away. Then he killed a buffalo, tore up the flesh, and offered some to the jackal. "Eat, comrade," the lion said. After the jackal had eaten, the lion ate too. Then the jackal took another piece and held it in his mouth.

"What's that for?" asked the lion.

"For my mate, who is waiting for me at home."

"A fine idea!" said the lion, taking some meat for his lioness. "Come, friend, let's stay on the mountaintop for a while and then go to your mate."

So they went to where the jackals lived and fed the jackal's mate. The she-jackal was so pleased with the meal that she forgot her initial fear of the lion. "Now I am going to take care of you both," the lion said. He took them to his den and settled them comfortably in a cave nearby.

After that, the lion and the jackal would hunt together while their mates remained behind to watch over the dens. Each day the lion and the jackal would bring back some food for their mates. As time went on the she-jackal and the lioness each had two cubs, and they all lived quite happily together.

One day, a strange thought crossed the lioness' mind. "My lion seems very fond of the jackal and his wife and young ones. Maybe he is too fond of the she-jackal!" She shook the thought from her mind and settled into a sunny spot for a nap. But she could not forget the awful suspicion that her mate loved the jackal's family more than his own. "Well," she thought, "I will torment the she-jackal and frighten her until she decides to leave."

Later that afternoon she began to taunt the jackal's wife, growling angrily and asking her why she and her cubs stayed there, why she did not run away? The lion cubs mimicked their mother and frightened the young jackals in the same way.

Later the she-jackal spoke to her mate. "Clearly the lion has hinted to his wife that he is tired of our company. Soon he may even try to kill us for his evening meal! Let us go back to our old home where we were safe!"

On hearing this, the jackal approached the lion. "Master lion," he said, "we have been here a long time. Those who stay too long outstay their welcome. While we were away, your lioness terrified my mate, asking her why she stayed and telling her to leave. Your young ones did the same to my young ones. If one does not like his neighbor, he should ask him to leave plainly. What is the use of all this harassment?" So saying, the jackal spoke this verse:

"When the strong roar loud,
the weak give ear.
Your mate threatens mine
and my trust turns to fear."

The lion listened, then turned to his lioness. "Do you remember how once I was out hunting for a week and then brought this jackal and his mate home with me?"

"Yes, I remember," she answered. "Do you know why I stayed away from home all that week?" asked the lion. "No, dear," answered the lioness.

"In trying to catch a deer, I had an accident and fell into the mud. I was stuck there for a whole week without food. This jackal saved my life. He was terribly afraid at first that I was tricking him, but he knew that I would die without his help.

"A friend who plays a helpful part,
however small and weak he be,
he is my heart, my flesh and blood,
a friend and comrade he.
Despise him not, my sharp-fanged mate!
The jackal saved this life for me!

"My mate, let yourself trust that love cannot be measured or weighed, nor can giving more love ever drain the source from which it comes. Rest assured that caring for our friends only enriches my love for you and our cubs."

The lioness made her peace with the she-jackal, and the four young ones grew to be as close as brothers and sisters. When their parents died, they did not break the bond of friendship, but formed a community as their parents had done. For many generations lions and jackals in a certain part of India could be seen living together peacefully, an example of loyalty and true friendship.

THE SERPENT
AND THE GARUDA

O nce upon a time a great multitude gathered together in Benares for a festival. Scattered among the closely packed crowds who came to watch the ceremonies were magic creatures called garudas and nagas.

Garudas have mighty wings, a lion's upper body, and an eagle's crowned head. They are traditional enemies of the powerful nagas and are often pictured holding snakes in their beaks.

Nagas, great serpent-like beings who live in the ocean depths and under the earth, guard natural resources and promote the growth of plant and animal life. In their head-crest shines a precious wish-fulfilling jewel.

Now it happened that in one very crowded spot at the festival a naga and a garuda were side by side, watching the celebration together. The serpent, not noticing that it was a garuda beside him, laid a hand on his neighbor's shoulder.

At the very moment that the garuda turned around to see whose hand this was, the serpent also turned to see who was standing so close beside him. For an instant the eyes of the two creatures met in friendship. In the next moment, both realized who the other was. The frightened serpent used his magical power to rise up in the air and fly away over the river, while the garuda gave chase close behind him.

Now at that time a hermit who was a great teacher was living in a leaf hut on the riverbank. The heat of the sun was so intense that he had put aside his garment made of bark and was cooling his skin with a wet cloth. As the serpent flew over the river, he saw the hermit bathing in the river.

"Surely I can find safety here," the serpent thought. Quick as a flash he assumed the shape of a brilliant green emerald and fastened himself to the bark garment. Only a breath away, the garuda saw where the serpent had gone, but out of reverence to the recluse he would not touch the garment.

"Sir, I am hungry," the garuda pleaded. "Look at your bark garment—that shining emerald is actually a serpent meant to be my dinner." To make the matter clear, he recited this verse:

"Concealed within a stone the wretched snake
has taken harbor for safety's sake.
Yet in reverence to what the holy wear,
though I am hungry I will leave him there."

The hermit looked deep into the garuda's eyes and touched his heart. "Reverence for holy things is admirable," he said, "but what benefit can it offer you if you only use it selfishly? Reverence for life, especially a life you have always sought to destroy, has far greater value."

Then the hermit touched the emerald gently and the serpent reappeared in its own form. "And you, serpent of the deep, had you not allowed fear to overtake your mind, your life may never have been in danger. Your strength lies not in your ability to hide, but in compassion.

"In true reverence for my holiness, I ask you both to live in that moment before you remembered to hate one another."

Both the garuda and the serpent decided to stay with the hermit and meditate on this great lesson for seven days. When this time was over, not one of the three spoke. The naga and the garuda flew away peacefully and have never been heard fighting since.

THE TWO BILLIONAIRES

Once upon a time in Rajagriha, a man of great qualities served as the king's treasurer. Known as the 'Billionaire', this man was worth eighty billion rupees. In Benares there lived another king's treasurer named Piliya whose worth was also eighty billion rupees. Piliya and the Billionaire had known one another for many years and were the best of friends.

Eventually Piliya of Benares fell into difficulties. Within a few short months, he lost all his property and was reduced to beggary. His former friends no longer recognized him. In his great need he left Benares with his wife and traveled on foot to Rajagriha to see the Billionaire, his last remaining hope.

The Billionaire embraced his friend and treated him as an honored guest. After Piliya and his wife had been given perfumed baths and had enjoyed

135

a good meal with their host, the Billionaire gently asked his friend the reason for his visit to the city of Rajagriha.

"I am a ruined man," answered Piliya. "I have lost everything and have come to ask your help."

"With all my heart! Have no fear on that score," said the Billionaire. "I have plenty for both of us, and it will give me great joy to share with you."

He had his treasury opened and gave forty billion coins to Piliya. He also divided his property, livestock and all, into two equal parts, and bestowed half of his entire fortune on Piliya. Taking his new wealth, Piliya returned to Benares and lived there in prosperity.

A few years later, a similar calamity overtook the Billionaire, who in turn, lost every penny he had. Casting about where to find help in his hour of need, he thought of how he had helped Piliya, giving him half of his possessions. Thinking that he might go to Piliya for assistance without fear of being turned away, he set out from Rajagriha with his wife and went to Benares.

At the entrance to the city he said to her, "Wife, it is not fitting for you to trudge along the streets with me. Wait here for a little while until I send a carriage with a servant to bring you into the city in proper fashion."

So saying, he left her under shelter and went on alone into town until he came to Piliya's house. There he asked to be announced as the Billionaire from Rajagriha, who had come to see his old friend.

"Certainly, show him in," said Piliya.

But at the sight of the Billionaire's condition Piliya neither rose to meet him nor greeted him with words of welcome. Instead he demanded what had brought him to Benares.

"To see you," was the reply.

"Where are you staying?"

"Nowhere, as yet. I left my wife under shelter and came straight to you."

"There's no room for you here. Take a handful of rice, find somewhere to cook and eat it, and then go away and never come to visit me again."

So saying, the rich man dispatched a servant with orders to give his unfortunate friend a few ounces of poor quality rice to carry away, even though on that very day he had threshed out a thousand wagonloads of the best rice and stored them up in his overflowing granaries. Piliya, who had taken forty billion coins from his friend a few years ago, now doled out a half quart of poor rice for his generous benefactor.

According to his master's wishes, the servant measured out the rice in a basket and brought it to the Billionaire, who debated with himself whether or not to take it.

"My ungrateful friend Piliya is breaking off our friendship because I am a ruined man," he thought. "But if I refuse his paltry gift, I shall be as bad as he is. The friend who scorns a modest gift outrages the basic idea of friendship; true friends do not measure the value of their gifts to one another. Therefore let me fulfill the bonds of friendship so far as I am able by accepting his gift of rice."

So the Billionaire tied up the rice in the corner of his handkerchief and made his way back to the entrance to the city where he had left his wife.

"What have you got, dear?" she asked.

"Our friend Piliya gave us this rice and washed his hands of us."

"Oh, why did you take it? Is this a fitting return for the forty billion you gave him?"

"Don't cry, dear wife," said the Billionaire. "I took it because I did not want to violate the principle of friendship. Why these tears?" Then he uttered this verse:

"If a friend plays the miser's part,
a simpleton is cut to the heart;

His dole of poor rice I will take,
and not for this our friendship break."

But still his wife kept on crying. Just at that moment a servant whom the Billionaire had given to Piliya was passing by. Hearing weeping he drew nearer. Recognizing his former master and mistress, he fell at their feet and with tears and sobs asked the reason for their coming to Benares. The Billionaire then told him their sad story.

"Keep up your spirits," said the man encouragingly. Taking them to his own quarters, he prepared perfumed baths and a meal for them. He gave them an honored place to sleep and did everything he could to make them comfortable. Then he let the other servants know that their old master and mistress had come. After a few days he marched the servants in procession to the king's palace, where they caused quite a commotion.

"What is the matter?" asked the king.

The servants told how their unfortunate master had been treated by his old friend Piliya. Then the king sent for the Billionaire and Piliya and had them brought before him and his ministers.

"Is it true," the king said to the Billionaire, "that your friend Piliya came to you when he was in need, having lost all of his money and property?"

"Yes, sire," said the Billionaire.

"And it is true that you gave Piliya forty billiion coins and half of all your property as well?"

"Sire," said the Billionaire, "when in his need my friend confided in me and came to seek my aid, I gave him half, not only of my money, but also of my livestock and everything else that I possessed."

"Is this so?" the king said to Piliya.

"Yes, sire," Piliya answered.

"And when, in his turn, your benefactor sought you out and told you about his desperate state, did you show him honor and hospitality?"

Here Piliya was silent.

"Did you have half a quart of poor rice doled out into the corner of his handkerchief?"

Still Piliya was silent.

Then the king took counsel with his ministers to determine what should be done. Finally, as a judgment on Piliya, the king ordered his ministers to go to Piliya's house and give all of Piliya's wealth to the Billionaire.

"No, sire," said the Billionaire, "I do not need what is another's. Let me be given nothing beyond what I formerly gave my friend."

Then the king ordered that the Billionaire enjoy his original fortune again. The Billionaire, accompanied by a large retinue, came back with his regained wealth to Rajagriha, where he paid his debts and put his affairs in order. He shared his riches with anyone who came to him in need, and his wealth increased beyond measure. After benefiting countless people through his generosity and kindness, the Billionaire passed away in peace.

THE TWO BROTHERS

Once upon a time a child known for his great compassion was born into the family of a wealthy landowner. He grew up to be a wealthy man. After his father died, he and his younger brother traveled to a village to take care of some of their father's business. There the elder brother received a thousand gold coins.

On their way back the two brothers ate a simple meal while they waited on the riverbank for a boat. The elder brother threw the last bites of his meal into the Ganges for the fish and dedicated the benefits of his action to the spirit of the river. The river spirit accepted this gift with gratitude, which further increased her merit and power. Then the older brother put his shirt down upon the sand, lay down, and went to sleep.

Unlike his older brother, the younger brother had a greedy nature. He wanted to steal the gold coins from his brother and keep them for himself. So he packed a sack of gravel to look like the sack of gold and hid them both away.

After they had boarded the riverboat and were nearing the middle of the river, the younger brother pretended to stumble against the side of the boat and dropped what he thought was the parcel of gravel overboard.

"Brother, the money has fallen overboard!" he cried. "What are we to do?"

"What can we do? What's gone is gone. Never mind about it," said the older brother.

The river spirit saw all this. She also saw that the greedy brother had mistakenly dropped the real money into the river. Pleased with the gift she had received through the actions of the older brother, she resolved to take care of his property. Using her powers, she made a big-mouthed fish swallow the parcel and then watched over it.

When the thief got home, he hastily undid the remaining parcel, chuckling to himself over the trick he had played on his brother. When he saw the gravel, he realized what he had done. In agony he fell over onto his bed, clutching the bedpost.

Just then some fishermen had cast their nets. Through the power of the river spirit, the big-

mouthed fish swam into the net, and the fishermen took it into town to sell. The townspeople
asked the price of the fish.

"A thousand pieces and seven pennies," said
the fishermen, still under the river spirit's power.

Everybody made fun of the fishermen. "We
have seen a fish offered for a thousand coins but
never a thousand and seven!" they laughed.

The fishermen then brought their fish to the
older brother's door and asked him to buy it.
"What's the price?" he asked.

"You may have it for seven pennies," they said.

"What did you ask other people for it?"

"We asked a thousand pieces and seven pennies from other people, but you may have it for
seven pennies," they said.

The older brother paid seven pennies for the
fish and gave it to his wife to prepare for dinner.
When she cut it open, there was the sack of gold!
She called her husband over to see this great
marvel. Looking at the sack, he recognized his
mark and knew it was his money. He thought,
"These fishermen asked other people the price of
a thousand pieces and seven pennies, but because the thousand coins were mine, they let me
have it for only seven pennies! How amazing that

things have worked out like this." And then he recited this stanza in verse:

"Who would believe the story, if he were told,
That a fish should be sold for a thousand
    coins of gold?
It cost me seven cents: How much I wish
that everyone could buy this kind of fish!"

After he had said this, he wondered how it came to pass that he had recovered his money. At that moment the river spirit hovered invisibly in the air, saying, "I am the spirit of the Ganges. You gave the remains of your meal to the fish and let me have whatever good came from that action. Therefore I have taken care of your property." Then she recited this verse:

"You fed the fish and gave a gift to me.
I remember this and your generosity."

Then the spirit told the older brother about the mean trick that his younger brother had played. "Now he lies in agony on his bed. For the thief there is no prosperity. But I have brought you your coins, and I warn you not to lose them again. Keep them all for yourself—do not give even a single coin to your brother."

Then she recited this stanza:

"There's no good fortune for the wicked
    heart,

and in my blessings the wicked one has
  no part.
He who cheats his brother out of his father's
  wealth
works evil deeds by craft and stealth."

With this, the river spirit returned to her home in the Ganges. "I see that I was wronged," the older brother said to his wife, "but this gold came to me through my father's generosity and I am glad to share it with my brother." And he sent his brother half of the thousand pieces.

Upon receiving the five hundred coins, the younger brother was filled with shame for his selfish and dishonest actions. He resolved to change his ways and practice generosity from that moment on. That very evening he went quietly to the poor people of his village and divided among them half of his five hundred coins. As a result of his practice of generosity, the younger brother learned the meaning of true prosperity and the joy from grows from unselfish actions.

GLOSSARY

alms money, food, or clothes offered to the poor

auspicious favorable; boding well for the future

Banyan an East Indian fig tree. Shoots from its branches take root and form new trunks over a relatively wide area.

Benares another name for Varanasi, a city in northern India

bestow to give or present as a gift

boon a welcome benefit; a request granted

bower a place enclosed by overhanging boughs of trees or by vines on a trellis

Brahma a chief of the Hindu gods often described as the creator of world systems

charger a horse ridden in battle

149

chariot a horse-drawn two-wheeled cart used in ancient times for war, racing, and parades

chase the hunting of game for sport

clamor to cry out loudly

dispatch send off or out promptly, usually on a specific errand, or on business

ember a glowing piece of coal from a fire

exile a prolonged living away from one's country or community, usually enforced

festoon a wreath or garland of flowers or leaves hanging in a loop or curve

Ganges a river in North India and Bangladesh, flowing from the Himalayas into the Bay of Bengal

guava a yellowish, pear-shaped fruit often used for jelly and preserves

hawking to advertise or peddle goods in the streets by shouting

Indra chief of the Thirty-three gods who reside in a heaven of the desire realm; associated with rain and thunderbolt; also known as Shakra

immunity freedom from something burdensome or otherwise unpleasant

jackal any of several wild dogs of Asia and North Africa, mostly yellowish gray and smaller than the wolf

jackfruit large, heavy fruit of an East Indian tree of the mulberry family, like the breadfruit

Kuber one of the Four Great Kings, Lord of Wealth, and ruler of the yakshas, usually benevolent beings who inhabit trees and mountains

kusha grass a creeping perennial grass, also known as Bermuda grass. In India kusha grass is used for meditation mats and is a traditional offering to a holy man. The Buddha sat upon a mat of kusha grass when he became enlightened at Bodh Gaya.

lot an object used in deciding a matter by chance, a number of these being placed in a container and then drawn or cast out at random one by one

lotus a tropical water-lily known in Asia for its beauty and purity; an ancient symbol of awareness and compassion

mail a flexible body-armor made of small, overlapping metal rings, loops or chains

mango a yellow-red oblong tropical fruit with a thick rind

mire wet, soggy earth; slush

multitude a large number of people or things

navigate to steer or direct, to plot the course for

nectar any very delicious beverage, like the sweet liquid in flowers used by bees in making honey

peerless having no equal

pomegranate a round fruit with a rosy red rind and many seeds covered with red, juicy, edible fruit

sari a long piece of cloth worn wrapped around the body with one end forming an ankle-length skirt and the other end draped scross the bosom, over one shoulder, and sometimes over the head. The principal outer garment of Hindu women

sheath to enclose in or protect with a covering

signet ring a finger ring containing a signet—a seal used as a signature—often in the form of an initial or monogram

sovereign the chief supreme in rank or authority; above or superior to all others

rebuke a sharp reprimand or reproof

retinue a body of followers attending a person of rank or importance

spoils property taken, usually in war, by the conqueror

steed a horse, especially a high-spirited riding horse

thoroughbred purebred

viceroy a person ruling a community, province, or colony as the deputy of a sovereign

vow a solemn promise or pledge dedicating oneself to an act, service, or way of life

wares any kind of goods that a merchant has to sell

White Umbrella a traditional symbol of honor, indicating royalty and associated with protection

winsome attractive in a sweet, engaging way

wish-fulfilling gem a magical jewel that fulfills all wishes for wealth and prosperity

yoke a wooden frame or bar with loops or bows at either end, fitted around the necks of a pair of oxen, etc. for harnessing them together

The Jataka Tales Series